MEMORY WAX

Also by Alan Singer: *The Ox-Breadth*
The Charnel Imp

MEMORY WAX

Alan Singer

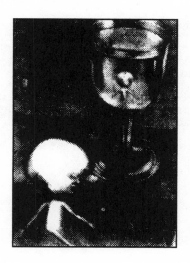

FC2
NORMAL

Published by FC2 with support given by the English Department
Unit for Contemporary Literature of Illinois State University and the
Illinois Arts Council.

Address all inquiries to: FC2, Unit for Contemporary Literature,
Campus Box 4241, Illinois State University, Normal, Illinois 61790-
4241.

Memory Wax
Alan Singer

ISBN: Cloth, 1-57366-014-0
ISBN: Paper, 1-57366-013-2

Cover/Jacket design: Todd Bushman
Book design: David Dean

"Jacket/frontispiece illustration "Human Embryo" is from *Histoire
Naturelle* (1781) by Jacques Gautier Dagoty, courtesy of the Getty
Center for the History of Art and the Humanities."

A portion of this work appeared under the title "Tonguetide" in
Western Humanities Review.

Printed on recycled paper

NATIONAL
ENDOWMENT
FOR THE
A R T S

For Nora, Alexandra and Anna,
indelibles.

What was there then in the wax that was so distinctly comprehended?

René Descartes
"Second Meditation"

It is impossible that bodies should be minds, yet it was believed that the thundering sky was Jove.

Giambatista Vico
The New Science

They did not lead Delta Tells in manacles to an iron cell where she could kneel beneath barred shadows and, under the harder gaze of a judge, press out a confession from her soft heart.

She had made a mad disarray of her hair, the better to hide the deputies from their fears when they looked at her, she thought. Crossed behind her back, her hands thrust out for the turnkey's rough grasp, she was already walking to the door. She was already nodding her head toward the swaying noose to show them that she would present no obstacle to her fate. If she could have removed the steps from her feet before she took them, so she would have shortened her path to the scaffold.

But no magistrate arrived with a formal clanking of chains. And those wary neighbors who had gathered to the sound of Delta's pealing voice would not take her into custody. The three neighborly wives, who stayed to hear Delta's story the second time through, sat calmly about her kitchen table, though it was within clear reach of the sharply serrated knife, the brightly pronged fork, the skillet that would ring with the weight of a sledgehammer, all still waiting to be washed. Sitting amid the crusted mixing bowls and freshly drained cutting boards, all the stained utensils that littered the cook's frantic circuit between the stove and the serving board, they listened to her confession and did not squirm.

They heard how she had grappled with the meal.

She said: at first she did not know how to hold the wriggling body against its movements or which was the softest part to pierce for the blood. What she held with one hand moved with the force of her other working hand, where it thrust only to strike bone or miss, chipping the enamel backsplash of the counter until she could not tell the movements of her hands from the life they gripped. So she made the knife move faster, slicker. Finally she knew that there was more movement in her self than she held in her hands and her hands were full of the spouting rubbery gouts, fatting her fingers, sticking to her palms, splashing the counter. The bowl was foaming to its rim of blood. Though she could not tell one piece from another, she advised herself that everything could be used in a stew.

The pot was big enough and she could cover it before the fouler smells boiled up into her nostrils, fingers of steam forcing her head back so that she couldn't see what she was about. She might have spilled.

The fire sputtered under the bubbling pot. The lid was unsteady but kept a steady, steamy pressure against her watchful eye. Everything, even the bones, like a shattered nest at the bottom of the pot, could be heard to simmer.

Finally, the escaping steam filled her eyes. It filled the room. When she moved, she became part of the expansion. No thoughts could enter such a diaphanous mind. Her only attachment to the world that stained her fingertips was the acid stink of a few singed hairs which pinched her nose and by that grip plucked her out of the sky of oblivion.

How had she set the table? The ring of bone china against the knottypine tolled in her ears still. Only one setting: the napkin rolled in its wicker holder; the two-tined fork; the toothy knife; the chair pulled out; each item of the setting mottled with the moist fingerprints of her tense attention to detail, though none of it had left any imprint on her mind. When she saw the table set, she widened her eyes as if she had just turned on her pillow toward the breaking light.

"It is a feast for a king," she told Brainard Tells, when she set the heavy iron pot before her husband's plate. And because he ate regally, with his back straight, his head high, though he was dipping into the very bottom of the pot, he must have believed that it was true.

When he was finished she saw that he had had no need of the napkin. He had licked himself clean. His lips glistened with satisfaction. She waited for the unwelcome smile to gnaw its way through the plumped mouth.

Then she spoke.

"Shall I be the regurgitation of the meal you cannot stomach, husband of my life?

"Once the servant of your banquet, let me now be the ticklish feather at the bottom of your clenched throat. If, when you are gathered into the arms of strenuous convulsions, you do not feel the violet heat of my embrace, then I have failed my sacred vow.

"Or can I draw the tide of your sickness with the lunacy of your good faith in me, knowing as I do that my words, empty footprints of my deeds, will soon be watered with your tears? They will leave a bright trail that is also the reflection of your downcast eye, wet as glass, malleable as wax.

"Rather, let me pick your teeth of the crime.

"I scratch a scent off your breath. I breathe it back to you. It is as thick as brushed hair. I scrape a fingernail off your tongue. For you, it is the bubble that has burst and left its effervescent tingle at the back of your throat. A fleck of blue iris sticks in the corner of your mouth like your own saliva. I hear the ache of your cracked tooth, the bone that is already crushed against your palate.

"Open your mouth to the fullest and I will name the colors painted with your appetite: pink of the fingertip poking your expanded waist. White of the eye in which your fright is congealed like a single roe from the chilly plate. Pale flush of the nose that is thrust against your larynx where you catch your breath. Yellow of the hairs that are stretched the unswallowable length of your throat. Pulling towards darkness, they are tuned against your feeble cough. These undying notes of sadness you have plucked with your own greedy fingers.

"Pink, white, pale flush, yellow and, finally, red of the bellowing mouth that shivers your esophagus with the sound of the baby's last tantrum. If you could open your livid mouth any wider, the whole shape of the infant head might disgorge with eyes, nose, hair, mouth, all the perfect likenesses of your sated self, so that you could see what you have done.

"You have eaten your own."

"What kind of a woman tells a story like that?" There was no one to answer where Delta Tells sat alone in the widening circle of those words, echoing against the silence of her thoughts. *She* was the pebble tossed into the ringing well. The emptiness of the house was all around her, deepened by the darkness that rounded every edge and corner, and made resonant by her concentration which, like a single black thread tangled at the invisible perimeter of her vision, pulled tighter against its entanglement.

"What kind of a woman tells a story like that?" her husband had asked. And the question had relayed back to her over the fluttering tongues of neighbors who had stood around his creaking barstool listening to his vehemence, watching him throw straight whisky on the fire in his stomach. They reported that the barroom door did not swing, glass did not tinkle while the told his side of he story. But, by the end, he held his belly as if he were muffling a fist at the door.

"You have eaten your own" she had said to him. His only answer had been to get his hat. His suspenders were down. The laces of his boots were untied. They lashed the boards he stamped on when he crossed the

threshold in pursuit, so he told her, of "more exotic fare."
Coal dust from his boots left ghostly steps behind him.

Delta had felt that the words were hardly out of her
mouth before he was out of the door. He might have
caught her tongue in the jamb. Instead she held it between her teeth, like the mouse by its tail.

When, hours later, she had to tell her part of it for
an audience of neighbors and strangers gathering around
the damp boards of her kitchen table, she had forgotten
that her tongue was still gripped so and her first word was
"ouch."

But now the room was empty again. She sat quietly
after the last of the listeners had gone. And nothing had
sounded so quiet since before she had swaddled the baby
for the first time in its starry blue quiltlet and taken it,
with all the planets, to her breast. Her hands in her lap
flexed against the emptiness that she could not fondle. Or
whatever nestled there could only be touched by the
airiness of the desire that was humming in her knuckles
and fingertips.

Nothing came to her. She had no words left to
conduct the movements that might have freed her from
such aching immobility. Everything she had said already
had been swallowed up by the incredulous eyes, the open
mouths of her impatient neighbors. But in the end the
eyes had borne no tears and the hungry mouths were
swallowed in turn by ungracious yawns. Now the emptiness it left inside her was expanding like steam off pavement. The soft sigh rose within her.

Like an involuntary ructation, it brought the words
to *her* mouth: "What kind of woman tells a story like
that?"

The morning after, the three wives, who had
heard it with their own ears, awoke with the story like a

sizzling thermometer under their tongues. They met as if in the feverish air of the physician's waiting room, mingling their symptoms with their breath. The story sweated from them in convulsive bouts of speech that left them tottering.

"Delta tells lies," she said, who found, in the wider eyes of her neighbors, the focus of her speech. The tension in her voice loosened her limbs into the embrace of the last empty seat. So she closed their circle, unsettlingly pronged though it was with the triangular arrangement of chairs around a kitchen table which bore no scars of the chef's knife and was not damp to the touch.

"Perhaps it is a fever laid like a suffocating blanket upon her thrashing mind that makes Delta Tells do the things she says. Delta Tells says that when she calmed the fluttering lid of the kettle she could feel the infant kicking against her fingertips. The same tremor she felt when she passed them over the telepathic drum of her pregnant belly.

"The steam rises in Delta's voice as she speaks, condenses into two droplets in her eyes. She wishes to embarrass me with the sight of myself doubly reflected there, my two mouths hanging open, about to disgorge a peristaltic darkness from the belly of each pendant tear. I blink before they fall and do not see.

"But when I close my eyes Delta is there, lifting the lid, stirring me up. Her hands drip. Her face bubbles with speech. There is surely a flame under her which has brought her words to a boil, too hot to taste.

"I blow on it with my own words.

"Delta tells lies, I say. Once, with the tip of the knifeblade a sparkling bead of perspiration at her Adam's apple, she swore to show us how her veins were flooded with the life of the gypsy seer.

"On that day the gypsy camp rose in a steady stream of smoke over the rim of our houses. Seen from afar it would appear that we were on the grill which exhaled the stench of all their greasy meals. That was only one reason for driving the gypsy off.

"But for Delta Tells it was far from enough. Standing straight as a tentpole in the center of debate, she promised to pierce herself if a single hand were lifted against the dusky tribe. Her blood would splash a divinatory map on the ground pointing the pathways of fate foretold for anyone who dared carry harm to the gypsy side.

"'The skins of gypsies, though dimmed with the smoke of their fires, could be wiped clear like a window,' Delta said, 'to view the life of the world. Each gypsy is a diorama under the skin where some scene of past and future events shimmers to be seen.' She said this. And she added that if we looked closely into that depth we would spy, amid the ant-like crowds, the tiny figurines of ourselves, stiffly stepping out of the past or into the future, as one watches a child playing in the distance, skipping over a rope.

"Our men, as they drove off toward the gypsy encampment that night, in an open-backed truck chiming with brandished hammers and picks, could have barely made out the sign of Delta's admonitory finger through the cloud of their exhaust.

"'Like soot from a candle blown out!' Delta sang after them. Then, turning upon the throng of women—we huddled behind for our safety—she pressed home the likeness of the candle like a spark to dry straw, setting us ablaze with fears of our husbands' foretold demise: 'The billowy smoke from the candle is only death arranging her skirts to accommodate more men,' said Delta Tells.

"But when the moon was snuffed out, the men returned on drunken choruses of song, kicking off the steps of gypsy dances like comfortable shoes, appearing swarthy in the dawn light, smelling of wood smoke and brine.

"Delta tells lies," she said, whose eyes rolled up two white fishbellies upon the surface of her speech.

"Delta Tells gives us the look of the mother who has just sopped the last bead of milk from her own nipple and then tells us how she wiped her husband's chin of the child. She puts her ten fingers on the table to show us what the pieces looked like after the knife. She flexes the blood against the raw knuckles turned up to our view in preparation for the waiting pot. She asks which of us would have noticed anything strange in such a stew. One finger is lifted in my direction.

"She tells us that the bottom of the bowl glistened brighter than her husband's teeth before she lifted the napkin to his mouth and kissed his lips with it. Her lips are parted to tell us this. But the words form a bubble, within which so much more that cannot be spoken stretches against the taut membrane of credulity. Her words are clear, but like the bubble that will burst, they swim upon the surface of nothing that we can see.

"Once before she taunted my eager eye with a mystifying depth.

"Her lips pronounced the word as if it were a sun-quenched grape to be caressed against the tongue until it yielded its juices without the pulp: 'Ramon. That is the name of your husband to be.'

"She spat it at me as I stepped from the doorway of my mother's house. 'Plant the seed of this knowledge in your heart,' she swore, 'and it will blossom in your breast. When he caresses you there he will feel it. He will tell you.'

"But I can tell you that I am married to Olaf, who spits continually as if there are grape seeds caught in his teeth."

"Delta tells lies," she said, whose face, turned from this talk, had gone ashen like the one cheek facing away from the hearth.

"Delta Tells kisses the air between us, better to imitate the sound of the broth sucking the lid back as she lifted it from the seething pot. 'The better,' she said, 'to taste.' Then she sizzled—sucking the mouthwater back between her front teeth.

"And so I realized that she was trying to feed us the child out of her own mouth, dredging the back of her throat for popping sounds to simulate the flame under the pot, filling her cheeks with shrill puffs of steam, flexing her tongue as if something struggled to escape from her speech. Its red claw could not strike hard enough to dislodge the lid from its tight rim. We who listened were as tight-lipped.

"Yet which of our mouths did not reluctantly

water, if only from the effort to keep it so tightly closed? Delta Tells would have known that the shut mouth becomes a deep well of saliva. In the depth of that well an appetite stirs, the shiver of an involuntary muscle with strength beyond saying. This is what she said.

"Delta's knowledge of the human mouth opens wide upon the field of human anatomy. She can tell us more about our bodily selves than ever we knew from our own innermost feelings, or by what warms to the touch of an exploratory hand. 'The woman's body is a book I can read,' she would say, licking her finger to turn a page.

"Yet we cannot believe her because she also tells us more than she knows. Because she tells us all and all we want to know.

"Once Delta told me: 'The days of a woman's flow are days to travel. A woman's legs should be in motion, pacing the bloodtide until it crests. A woman who walks continuously during this time eventually comes to a place in her body like the silted floodplain at the river's mouth. There, if she stoops to feel the slow breath of dampness coming off the suspiring ground, she will know it is a loam of fertility. If she will plant her seed there, it will blossom, and the fruit of the tree will reach down to the ground, easy for the plucking.

"Taking Delta Tells at her word, I cast myself off from the mooring of my bedpost on the first flood. I was adrift in the motions of walking for six days. I walked not far, but tirelessly to the back of the rocky yard and back.

"And in the narrow path of my march the red mountain clay turned gradually to sand under my shoes. At last, as the earth gave way beneath my grindstone gait and the mountains flowed to the sea, I felt a tremor within, a single grain of sand moving aside—like a stone from the mouth of a cave—permitting the seed to pass.

"But even that richly cultivated soil yielded only the two knocking stones of my husband's gonads, giving barely a spark to the laborious pick where it rained upon barren ground.

"Delta tells lies."

The wind was another tongue thrust into his mouth when Brainard Tells shouted back over his shoulder for his wife to go home. The bluster that had blown him out of the house stormed back at him from the whistling dome of the night sky. Delta Tells had pursued him through the violently flung door, casting after him a string of women's names, hoping to snag his recognition, hoping to turn his head, to hear the other woman's name in his eyes. But her words, with the wind, were driving him further away.

She spread her arms as if she held the corners of the thunderous black sheet flapping in his ears. Though his back was still turned, she stretched her arms wider as if to show him that by drawing her hands together she might wrap them both in a suffocating shroud. But she preferred to let the wind fly like a black cape over her shoulder, to descend on him again as if the whole sky were her wingspread.

Through the din she implored him to wipe his mouth. The white napkin blew off her fingertips like the last candle to go out. She offered her sleeve. The hand that pushed out of it flew against his turned shoulder. A blind bird striking the pulled shutter. She hurled a stony fist.

"...think...me...mad," the words lashed from Brainard Tells' mouth, his head bounding wildly on the dark wave of one shoulder, drifting out of her reach. Now she realized that she could only see him when he turned his face toward her, though it did not turn his body. Nothing else caught the fitful light of the moon like phosphorescent fish scales strained through the blowing nets of wind.

And because he turned his back on her again, because he was walking on, she had to put out her arms to follow him. It was as if she herself were the drowning victim. And for the first time she felt the wind as a tempestuous depth in which she could lose her own head like any flotsam under a sudden swell. She could be swallowed up, clamped beneath the tongue of storm, silenced under its roar.

Her hair was already flying around her ears as if spread upon a watery surface. She was already the victim, face down in a depth that would never throw back her reflection.

So the wail that finally went up from her lips was a cry for "help." The word, as stark in its utterance as the white arm of the victim sliding beneath the surface, was nevertheless blustery enough to blow bubbles in the husband's blood.

When she saw his belligerent face swimming back to her, it was with the satisfaction of the fisherman hauling his net to the surface.

"Your hand," was all she heard before she dropped to her hands and knees. She flattened herself upon the ground. She let the sound of the wind rise above her cry, knowing that he would find himself on the brink of it so suddenly that he couldn't save himself from the fatal precipice, his will lost with his balance.

Fallen into her arms, he did not understand how she had deliberately proffered this depth. She wanted to hold his head under it until his breath was gone into her arms, inflating the pulse of her embrace. They struggled together under the slapping tail of the wind, but it was her hand that struck the blows against his face, that made the red of his cheek bloom in the bursting bud of the windy night, a concussion of color throbbing against the shut eyelid.

Inside that darkness he felt her moving as if she were the worm uncoiling in the jelly of his own sleeping eye, waking him out of a dream so fearful he could not force the lid open to see. Was he awakening or was he already tamped firmly under a man's weight of shoveled earth? She was already inside his clothing. Her fingers were all the movement the worm needed to penetrate his skin. Once inside, the wriggling life of the worm took over his whole body in convulsions that she felt reciprocated first around her own neck. And for response, she gripped him tighter.

They would have been taken for two copulating snakes if the wind had come upon them like a stumbling blind man. But it was the blindness of their own struggle that so infuriated their movements. And the wind kept them off balance, buffeting their blows with the bulk of a larger and more violent, phantom, body. Neither relinquished the grip on the other. Neither could free arms or legs from the flexure of the irate will.

But while the pain was a helpless bird in the net of the husband's groin, the wife's head fluttered free from his grip on her throat. She bared teeth against his powerful wrists, biting into the blood that ran along the bone. He hadn't realized that she was kicking as well. Her feet sank into his kidneys, stones hurled into mud. A loose shoe caught the back of his head, sharp as a fingernail digging to get underneath the scalp.

And something was pulling the top of Brainard Tells' head. His mind was bunched at the roots of his hair. Like a knotted rope-end pulled sharply through the hole in a stiff board, the thought hit him in the top of his brain that she was capable of far greater violence than he. Nor, he realized, was the wind her match for all its diabolical fury.

And with her lips she was telling him that his thoughts were correct—even though she had placed her mouth over his own, before he could hear her speak the words, before he could cry out himself for help.

Then she might have put a knife in his groin, the turning of her wrist was so sharp, the grip of her fingers so tight, the full length of her so swiftly discovered where she had forced him inside herself—the one indrawn breath in all this bellowing weather—a hush of bodily warmth closing over him. The slap of a drowning wave.

His fingers lifted from indentations in her esophagus where he had found the shrillest notes of the instrument. But now he was dancing by himself, without the accompaniment of any rhythmic partner. The breath throbbed within like a drum. His feet struck out at the

shiny planks of the dancefloor too far below. His arms
flailed in the air above his head. He was being dragged by
a melodious current that only flowed within him, toward
her, where she waited with wide arms to enfold him in a
silence so muscular that he could have been convulsively
swallowing his own tongue.

But he now realized that *she* swallowed *him*. She
clenched the last beaded drops of his physical reserve
within her as tenaciously as the grain of sand holds the
pearl that is hardened against it.

The strength of her embrace flexed in her legs. Her
legs were joined like arms behind his back. There, in the
small of his back, the place which was only as wide and as
tender as the bulging eye of astonishment—but where his
own eye would never contemplate the invisible leash
attaching each man to an uncertainty as hard as the
rusted, iron clasp of the leash itself—there, she held him
with the heel of her foot.

"You have eaten your own.

"You who are my husband should believe what I
say.

"I have cooked for you. Your stomach is my massage. My fingers can touch your appetite. A pea pod does
not yield more easily to the pressure I exert. Because we
are wedded by the osmotic vows murmured along intestinal passageways, my words should be to you as a porous
membrane through which you might pass like like an
eager sweat. Believe me:

"Or, if you insist, consider the alternative. Listen
to the thoughts that harbor your hope like the echo in
resonant stones. But remember you must break your voice
upon those stones to hear it coming back to you.

"So listen. When you put your ear to the wall of
this house does it ring with the cries of the cradle? Is the

silence not like the sound of the seashell when, drawing it from your ear, it is the ear that seems to fade? Look for your own child. Search the rooms of this house. Is there room in my eyes for the look you are giving me now?

"So, at least I have captured your attention. Do the criss-crossed lines of grief in my face *not* flex the spider's sudden agitation at the center of the web?

"Or is my speech too florid for an occasion which evokes damp, overcast weather and holds you in its clammy spell?

"Nevertheless, I ask you to believe me when I say the words: You have eaten your own. They are in my mouth as warm and salubrious as when they were no more than the curl of your tongue against the roof of your own mouth, trying to swallow.

"Watch my lips, and when I have spoken enough, you may find yourself unable to keep from swallowing."

There had been other women from the beginning and all of Delta Tells' senses had quickened to the chase. Delta Tells remembered the first scent of suspicion that wafted off her husband's bare back. His perspiring shoulders tilted above her were the steep incline to which she abandoned herself in the act of love. Now memory was the inertia of that slippery slope.

But this time she remembered herself as a dog, all the tumbling life of her aroused body at once convulsing in her nostrils with the recognition of another woman's presence—her damp hair, her hot breath, the quivering heat of her narrow waist, the urgent secretions of her pelvis, gathering in Delta's concussive consciousness the force of a violent sneeze.

And like the dog, Delta had whimpered. Like the dog, she had felt the shock on her face, drawn out the length of a wet and trembling snout. Like the dog, she shoved her snout into the blushing darkness of her master's groin.

There the deeply impregnated scent of the other woman was flexing a muscular presence. As from a clenched fist, the mystery woman's scent unfurled stiff, square fingertips of provocation, sculpting the expression of rage that would have snarled upon the face of the dog.

So when Delta lifted her human face toward her husband's silvery, moon-shaped smile, she gave voice to the buried bone itself. Sharp, broken at one end, sucked dry, it would stick in his throat.

"So you are unfaithful to your wife, the mother of your child. So, you are such a man. And such a man deserves only to be soaked in the burning sweat of his guilt like a body dipped into molten wax. So, you should be shed of your life in the perfect likeness of your lascivious skin. So should your death become the cruel mirror of your life."

She backed away from the expression that was lengthening on the husband's face like a narrow hallway measured off by her own footsteps. The shadow of a wall collapsed upon him. The floor might have been pulled out from under him, she had moved so deftly, leaving him to grope for balance, his arms out in front of him, tipping him into the plummet of the somnambulist's rude awakening. But she had taken only two steps backwards. The discrepancy between the short distance she had moved and the yawning space through which he was now falling inspired *her* to smile back at him.

"You will come no nearer to me," she thrust her jaw at him. He reached for the lashing rope-end of speech where it snapped out of reach and he fell from the bed.

Because she was now looking down at him, she could believe that the expression of grief already wrinkling his face would crumple compactly into the palm of one hand. The palm of her hand darkened to the intensity of the oily walnut shell clenched around its softer meat.

Though he was still wearing his pants, they were gaping when he raised himself to all fours. The smile fallen from his face reappeared in the loose mouth of his trousers—turned into a frown, like a sliver of moon that had tumbled end over end. The tongue of his belt panted between his heavy thighs. He simply waited for her to speak again.

She gave a command. "Then you must tell me how she is different from myself. Give me the measure of her on my own body so that I will know always where she is, so she will always be within my reach. Tell me what I need to know.

"She is smaller than myself? Would her head fit into the soft pit of my arm, like a trembling egg in a nest? Does her belly reach the prominence of my breasts? Her pelvis is a tighter pair of forceps for your heated brain? Do her lips protrude more voluptuously than my own? Or would they shrink into my own moistening smile like the innermost petals of the fully dilated blossom?

"You should know how to answer my questions. Yet you only stare up at me as if I were *she* standing before you for the very first time. Do you ask her if you can come closer? Does the tilt of her chin signify how precarious is the balance of your desire? Is it the precipice upon which you now stand, like a dumb animal driven forward by some scent loosed into the wild air? And you're already shaking because even the weight of your whole body will not be enough ballast against the storming of a flared nostril?

"Do I describe it well? Then let me lead you further. Trust me enough to take this hand."

She stooped, and for the first time she was at his level. Her lips grazed his lowered lashes as fish feed on waving grasses at the bottom of the stillest pool. He felt the suction of her imploring speech as if he were the snail being pried from its green rock.

And he knew it was an aqueous world because his eyes were brimming and his nose, full of his heavy breathing, seemed to pull his head beneath the surface of the light and sounding ambience that was slipping out of his reach leaving him breathless even as she hauled him to his feet. Only his pants sank beneath him as she drew him up into the eddying circles of a dance step. He was compelled to follow, a circumspect angler marking a trail of bubbles on the surface of the water. But when he tried to speak himself he felt the hook in his own mouth where the words throbbed against the clutch of his throat. He knew that to prod them into utterance then would be to taste the full metallic thrust of the barb into the center of his brain, which was already as soft as roe and brimming with its salty sting.

Naked, docile, compliant as a good student, Brainard Tells danced her steps. With each stride he took in a word of instruction from her lips again, as if she had him by the tongue, playing out the tension of that line to the darting rhythms of her own outrage. She said: "This is the way a man should behave with his wife because there is no other woman whom he would embrace. She fills the reach of his arms like a ship to safe harbor. The spice of the voyage in her hair is the cargo he has vouchsafed. He is a man for whom the bodies of other women are merely glassy resemblances to a truth that does not brook comparisons unless to break them, showing their fragility for what it is.

"But now, even worse than flaunting resemblances, you have made a difference by your actions. Therefore everything you want from me must be different too, from this moment on."

The large bowl of oranges blazing on the sun-splashed sill appeared as a blossoming yellow blur. This was a natural partner to the dancing motion itself which was pulling him into tighter and more claustrophobic circles of dizziness. So he did not notice how closely she had drawn him to the window.

Nor did he notice how the bright and curved, serrated blade of the fruit knife that she seemed to pluck from the bowl and thrust deftly into the pulp of his own groin in actuality sank up to its hilt in the thick skin of a plump naval orange. The slap of crenulated citrus skin was the only blow that he had felt to his own body, though the pale juice which spurted from beneath the silver handle of the knife resembled the squeezings of a more gruesome sensation which, he only now understood, she had deliberately spared him. The cool, white hand that still gripped the shuddering orange between his legs made the knife handle wiggle in its resting place.

How had she moved so quickly to substitute the bulging fruit for his own anatomy? How did he not see the difference between the shape of the knife and the sensation that was thrust upon him like its distorted shadow?

What Brainard Tells had not seen with his own eye submerged into a mystery that would remain locked within the vaults of physical sensation, a morsel whose digestion dissolves away the image of what one desired. The contact with teeth and tongue is the advent of a long night that will only be shed—like the snake's skin—by the sheath of a quavering bowel.

The words of apology were curds of a cold porridge clenched in Brainard Tells' throat. But they stuttered forth, imparting a sour taste to every motion of his mouth: "I am your husband. I will be faithful. I will not blemish my skin with the touch of another. My perfection will be yours to mark. It is every husband's duty and rightly every wife's pleasure."

His head snapped back from the last word of this pledge, so taut had it been drawn between the two sets of concentrating eyes. With the snapping of the thread the colorless beads of mutual recognition which had been strung upon it flew into the oblivion of a spacious and densely furnished room.

The mine shaft resonated louder in the ear canals of the miners as they went deeper into their homes at night. Their bent legs still felt the compression of the earth which they had borne on their backs all day, a tension never to be fully sprung from their stride. A night shift went in behind them, but no one looked back to see the enormous steel elevators descend into the hole. No one waved. Each man, walking away from the sulphurous rim of the hole, carried a bullet-shaped silver lunch case under his arm. Each man nosed his front door as if it were only another clod of earth to be pushed aside. Each man sat down to wait for the smells of the kitchen to descend around him, breathing deeply, as if he were finally coming up for air.

The hilly streets lined with modest tin-roofed bungalows sounded under nightly mountain breezes like tedious fingers tapping the drumhead of a rickety tabletop. The lights burning behind waxy casements would blow out like guttering candlesticks when the weather breathed heavier and the night sky pressed upon the valley. But even the valley was high where it lay between upthrust peaks, a tiny gasp sucked back from a precipice. Two roads departed from this rocky cleft and ran as fast as tumbling water to the depths of green countryside below, throwing back reflections of calm, flat vistas to soothe the tottering mountain eye.

Though at the changing of the shift they passed one another without making a sign, each man on top of the earth kept up a furtive communication with the ones still working below. Whatever his preoccupation with the upper world, he always had one ear to the ground. So he always tapped a heavier foot than was necessary, to the music a woman might be humming to herself like a hat pulled over her ears; he deliberately knocked a book from the shelf where he leaned his own loud voice on a sharp elbow, telling a funny story to the circle of laughing faces; instead of walking, he leaped from room to room throwing his weight out in front of him like a shot. Each man did what he could to keep up a rhythm for his friends below. For when they fell into that rhythm, it danced them around each other's faces until above and below became a perfect pirouette, the separate movements held together like night and day by the forgetful momentum of the earth's rotation.

When the shifts changed again at sunrise, the ones who went down held the brightening morning air in their lungs until the descent of the elevator car was complete.

When at the bottom of the shaft they breathed out, they said they saw the day dawn above their heads like struck phosphorous.

The skeptical woman, peering into her husband's eyes, would wonder to see how his pupils were so contracted by the darkness of his daily labor. But her ever more credulous arms around her husband's waist would soon be warmed by that underground sun, radiating back until it glistened on her skin as brightly as it shone in his eyes. He says this light gives him nimbleness when he moves deeply inside her, nudging the eel-head of darkness where it makes a home of her most shadowy want. Her eyes, filled with his shadow, can see nothing from that abyss.

So the wives and the mothers knew the deepest regions of their desire only second hand as an echo from an undulant and paradisical valley that can only be touched in the thinnest, most inaccessible membrane of sensation, by calling out to it, over empty space, and listening.

She says to her lover: "My own." She hears herself say it like sound struck from a distant rock. The words dented with the imprint of all they have touched without fingertips.

Then she pushes against her husband's damp chest as if she were the one moving the earth. But when he breathes, his breath (falling upon her ears like spadefuls of black earth) echoes with the stronger conviction that *he* has never been deeper. The harder she presses upon his breastbone the further his levered reach inside her, until at last she seems to gasp the air from that coveted depth herself—but the breath is engorging the ecstatic gash of her mouth like the tail of the snake, choking the orifice that feeds its most wriggling ways.

When the new shift begins, some of the women watch the grey elevators descend and think they know a hydraulic pleasure in their loins, stepping back from a rumbling of steel cables and the clang of the earth's lid. But all day they hear nothing more from the earth. There are no voices ringing in the kitchen drains where she waits for an answer to this sensation in her loins which has lasted all the way home. Neither will the toilet speak to her from its clutched throat of porcelain. There is no shiver in the floorboards when she does not tread on them. She waits patiently, but in vain, for a caravan of tiny glass elephants to tinkle on the tabletop which is receptive to the lightest footfall in the house.

Yet when he is home again, she sees how her husband's ears are pricked by more than the clink of crockery in the kitchen sink. He busies himself behind the closed door of the bathroom without ever pulling the chain. Sitting silently beside his wife, the husband suddenly drops his eyes to the floor. And he is forever calming the backs of the elephants as if to head off a stampede.

The man puts his foot to the floor as another puts a glass to the wall and hears a voice coming towards him on the crest of a wave. The woman only knows how to stand upon her foot in unsteady anticipation of where her body will lurch next.

A world turns beneath them both, but only for the man does the round surface turn up to him like his own reflection down a well.

The flush had not faded from Brainard Tells' face since the words of the previous night had flared in his head: "You have eaten your own." The match-head gleams hottest when it has consumed the flame.

In the deepest shaft of the mine one man's light was another man's way. The underground men worked in teams of two, one with a pick, one with a bucket. The fall of the pickhead echoed in the scraping of the bucket across the scored floor of the tunnel. The avalanche of fractured stone broke again, as each bucket was hoisted over the loud rim of a squat trolley car that received it. Then the sag of the track answered the call of the shattering coal car with a groan, and a click and a slurring sound of metal on metal.

As no sound went unanswered in the rising din of this activity, so each man had his counterpart in the teamwork that took them deeper into the anthracite forest. Moving in twos through petrified darkness, each man became accustomed to the swing of four hands, the gait of four feet, the ominous girth of the invisible body that lurched between them.

It was written in the *Safety Manual* that if two men were always together no one would ever be lost. No man would stray into solitary darkness apart from the ring of shadowy footsteps. No man would suddenly have to wonder to himself if the air were filling with an invisible gas. The warning would spark in the alerted eyes of his partner before it could breathe them both into the combustion chamber of all delayed reactions. And in the worst case, should the roof of coal collapse behind him, and with the swiftness of the lamp blown out, no man would have to lie flattened alone in that compacted vacuum space without a breath of conversation. Even if it swallowed them whole, the toothy maw of the cavern would never shut completely over men who lifted each other's spirits upon the prying seesaw of a joking tongue.

Brainard Tells, helmeted, goggle-eyed, cinched up in his utility belt, breathed upon the dim mirror of darkness that he hollowed out with his pick.

"Seeing is believing," he said to his silent partner.

But his words only pulsed inside the respirator mask. The sound of the pick thickened in his ears, making his head as heavy as the weight in his hand. It reverberated with each blow, as if the wall were striking him back.

The partner startled to see Brainard Tell's whole body collapse beside him. The pick, impaling the wall, might have flung the worker off the end of its handle, it was still so shivering with the force of the blow that broke the human grip on it. But the victim was not fallen into a heap where the partner dropped his eyes to see.

Brainard Tells balanced purposefully upon his knees below the white glimmer of the pick handle, the better to see his own hands delving into the flow of a turbulent darkness. Coal dust, rising from the floor of the shaft like a secret spring, issued in an intensity that was invisible to the eye but as certain to the touch as a wet hand on a dry shoulder.

Dredging something to the surface? Cupped like phosphorescent minnows in his open palms? Or was he blotting up the darkness with the absorbent sleeve of his denim jacket, stretched between the gripped cuff and the jut of the elbow?

The men who had grouped themselves raggedly around him now gathered their lanterns together like bright beads onto a looping thread, tightening the circle of their attention.

There, under the converging rays of scrutiny, the hub of a wheel began to turn, gripping everything on its nauseating circumference in a spell of centrifugal force that held them motionless.

Raising himself from what could have doubled for the posture of prayer, snapping his shoulders back, like they were the white-gloved hands atop the magician's spread cape, Brainard Tells drew himself back to reveal— where his shadow would have been most densely compacted—the gleaming viscosity of an internal organ. Or it seemed, washed as it was in the hand-spilled light, that a heart beat nearby, transmitting its urgent, irregular rhythm through the taut membrane of their collectively held breath.

In the span of his spread knees was a declivity, a glistening edge. Delving over the edge again, Brainard Tells' own hand touched the throbbing curve of bladder shape or liver size.

Whatever else they had expected, the surrounding faces all opened at the same time around the protruding shape of the one incredulous word.

"Egg?"

"Eggs," he echoed. And he showed them by cuddling one away from the nested covey, into the cradle of his open palm. It was a melon's size, but black, smooth, harboring a shine that glinted recognition in the goggle eyes of all who peered—as if over the bobbing rail of a ship at night—into a blinking abyss.

Not one note of alarm sounded above the huddled breathing when, with a careful hand, Brainard Tells set the egg on end, and with the balanced swiftness of the other hand unsnapped the hammer from his heavily riveted utility belt. Propping the egg with one hand, he held the head of the hammer above it as if focusing rays of his concentration through the lens of a glowing magnifying glass. Then there was compounded into the flat head of the hammer both the hard clarity of the glass and the force of the shattering blow.

But where the hammer gained entry to the black egg, there was no interior. And that outside was no shell because its shattering bits contained only their outward trajectory. The hand that had balanced the egg held only its empty grip.

Then the fingers clenched implosively. They would have been fast enough for the darting tip of the lizard's tail, before it flickered out of sight of the encircling watchers. But there was as little pinched between Brainard Tells' straight forefinger and thumb as if they had snuffed the flame of a candle.

The clustering eyes stared into that vanishing point until it weighed with concentration as heavily as the dense bodied reptile they would have loosed from the somnolent mystery of its ancient shell.

The proffering of a second egg elicited the ringing aura of a lighter sledge-hammer. The hand that lifted the shaft of the hammer sought a way to soften the blow at the point of its hardest impact, as if what was dealt to the outside of the egg could be spared the inside. The motion of Brainard Tells' arm sought the thinness of a fingernail picking the shell from the viscosity it floated upon. He reached for what writhed beneath the shell but without turning up any slippery flipper of existence or scaly edge that might be pulled deftly into a view struck so hard with the light of expectation. There was only the pull of the hammerhead through the sucked breath of the stroke.

Another empty explosion. Unclutchable puff of

choking dust, foul breath of the hammerblow, pulling grimaces from beneath pinched nostrils as if dredging the odor of rotten eggs.

But nothing rotted where there was no thing.

"A thing," whispered Brainard Tells, "must be there, even if it does not appear to be. Or wouldn't we be bound to believe in appearances all unto themselves?"

Three hands fell on his own where he had already selected the third egg, his thought as heavy upon it as the ringing steel. Suddenly the struggle in his arms summoned the vast, impatient motion of the reptile shedding its skin. Brainard Tells wanted the mallet thump of the thirty-foot tail in the thrust of his own back against the restraining grip of the six burly hands. He wanted heaviness beyond the flung weight of himself to toss his captors into air. He wanted the scale of the whole dinosaur life to amaze them with the lucidity of his protest, like anything brought to light with the sparkling blows of a shovel.

Instead they buried him. Beneath the hurled weight of six strapping miners' bodies Brainard Tells lay flat. He achieved in his own abandoned physique the impact he had so clearly foreseen in the aim of the first hammerblow. Compressed by such solidity of purpose he experienced the blind and vacant inertia of the fossil itself.

Those who had heard it with their own ears, carried the story like a lump in their throats. It was something for the listeners to press upon with tender fingers, feeling the weight of inquiry more acutely than what bulged against their touch.

"Delta tells lies," she said, whose mouth was still full. She picked her words more daintily than fish bones from the soft mash of her speech.

"Delta Tells says she knows more about her child now than we, when we only fondle the form of our own.

Delta's lips come together when she says this. I think that for her to whisper such a terrible secret she must fashion a kiss. But then I understand that it is only to make the sound come hotter from her lips.

"She says, 'Ssss.'

"And from that sound I know her eyes are in the pot, staring back at me to make me see how her pupils float like beaded grease in the stew. She wants to knock me off balance, to stir me in.

"What she whispers is: '*Brainard*', and as she raises the volume, I can hear from her pinched lips how they brought him up from the pit, though I know it all already.

"Delta's voice, thin as an eggshell, makes me feel her pick at me all the more.

"'They raised him flat,' she says. 'They had to hold him down to bring him up. But I knew what it meant that his legs were spread and his knees were bent.

"'Wide berth for the midwife!' she joked, because she knew I had heard about the eggs. 'A man has eggs too,' she said, 'but they're cuddled up in his head, safe in the nest. So how can he ever be delivered of them?'

"Seeing his legs, (as Delta Tells said she did), canted and spread wide on the floor of the lift and picturing the egg as it was described to her, black, melon-sized, bullet shaped, shiny as sweat, she asked me how this narrow man could have passed it through the length of his body without the kind of pain that shakes the toilet to the ground. She laughed, she said, at the body's miracles.

"But I know that Brainard was lying down when they brought him up because they'd knocked him harder than they meant to. And whoever put his knees up that way was only clearing space on the lift for the remaining eggs, piled to his knees so that anyone could see what it was all about.

"Delta tells lies," she said, who shows her teeth behind every word, under every flouncing ruffle of lip.

"Delta Tells says a man's body has no place to hide. That's what makes a woman the deeper creature. And that's why his fascination with her is a hole. She tells us that we don't think enough about the fact that a mine shaft is a hole as well. 'And in your heads too,' so she throws it up to us!

"I know she is trying to make me feel something in my legs where they are parted in the breathless seat of the chair. She is already there before I can think about it, talking. Because, of course, her uttering mouth is a hole.

"Out of a hole in the ground she says we shall now see how neither is her husband whole in his own mind. She prods in the form of a question: 'A man rises from the deepest pit and can't be talked to? And anyone who talks about what happened there below can't be understood? Under this weird moon, wouldn't anybody know enough to raise an eyebrow, to smile back?'

"But the mining men who saw what happened down below have talked a bounty to me. They've seen a man throw fits before in their lives and don't call it anything more than that. 'Exhaustion... distraction...wits at an end...weighted with an undue burden of woman...a terror, a tragedy, a trial,' are the words they use. And I know what they mean."

"Delta tells lies," she said, whose eyes pool with the depth of feeling as she sounds it, every word a pebble tossed closer to the middle of the pool.

"Delta Tells says she has dropped her husband into the riddle of a widening sea. There he shrinks in proportion to the expanding ring of his thoughts. She tells us to see him ("in his sea") like a beady iris—awash in a sudden swell of eyewhite—tiny, hard, black pit of fear pulped from the juices of life in the ripeness of his wide-eyed terror.

"'That's him', she says, without pointing. She says, 'Truly out of his depth.' Then she says to me, 'Perhaps you'll try, just one pink toe.'

"But there is nothing more I want to know from Delta Tells. And she does not know that I myself am a good swimmer, even if this mountain town holds no body of water deeper than a sunny rain puddle. And the man she speaks of stands high enough to her that she would drown if he were the river she swam in."

The authorities took Brainard Tells' deposition from his rattling infirmary bedside. His testimonial voice shook as violently as if the underground struggle reverberated yet in his bones.

But now it was the *absence* of the child he was trying to sound with his heavy words. He spoke from the resonant hollow of a conviction that his wife may not have been merely telling him a story.

Three official men stood bedside with heads cocked as though to dispel a ringing from their ears. Each darkened his own bright tablet with a shroud of notes. Because Brainard Tells had devoutly wished to see each of his words throw a shadow, like drops of blood in the snow making a trail straight to the scene of the crime, he warned the note-takers that their task might require any number of backward steps.

Stiff white coat, five- pointed silver star, pin-striped suit (with goggles hung around the neck). These were the three signs under which the husband hatched his worst fears. Each of the witnesses had heard the story before from the wife's side, though neither doctor, sheriff, nor Superintendent of Mines knew the sound of her voice. Perhaps because Brainard Tells appeared (in a rhythm of white wavelets) to be bobbing upon the surface of something larger than all visibility, his heaving shape under the infirmary sheets was preferable to the small, invisible voice of the woman.

Brainard Tells said he could only tell them what he *didn't* know with certainty, since his own knowledge was compassed by the chipped circumference of a dinner plate.

But he did know the tone in his wife's voice, like a brittle black leg scratching inside a chrysalis. He knew the look on her face when she spoke to him, like mysterious moisture inside a sealed glass. He knew the touch of her that came like something silken pulled sharply between the legs.

He repeated her words, made her faces, reaching out to his audience with her hand gestures. He told them word for word what she had said to him, counting the medicinal spoonfuls of incredulity on the back of his tongue. Swallowing or regurgitating? He could not tell himself.

Doctor, sheriff, Superintendant did not rest their pencils since it meant they would not have to meet the witness's eye. Wrapped in this rigidly concentric activity, each scribbling man stood like a separate pillar, as if some ominously echoing roof depended upon it.

But only the patient's iron bed threatened to collapse under the commotion of so much unburdening speech. Because when he was done with what she had to say, Brainard Tells found that there was more within him. Buried so much deeper, it required a much more gutteral labor. So the voice had to heave against the stubborn weight of what lies at such depths. And it became raspy as the prying tip of the shovel against its buried rock. And there was suction in it too, as if the shovel were a wriggling finger in the digger's own ear at the moment of unearthing.

"Delta Tells has ever spoken of things the doing of which would have brought her to the docket before this. Against me especially she has made threats that could only have been imagined out of deeds already as dark.

"Or how else could she know the things she says?" he asked. "How does she know how to find the path where a thread-like muscle follows the descent of the nerve into the scrotal sac and snags it—taut as a fish on the line—so that if you pierce him there with the barest glint of the knifeblade a man's whole generation falls away, like the heaviest limb of a fruit tree struck off in its moment of bearing?

"Or how else could she know that if it is to be a needle, it needs at least six inches, to pass though the pulsing temple as through a cork panel, to extinguish the eye from behind—thus blinding even the medical man who might contemplate the victim's bloodless agony from the mirroring depths of the open iris?

"Or how else could she know how to count the ribs—quick fugitive steps—to the place where, between prying fingertips, the damp skin can be palpated, made supple and thin until the mouth of an artery is coaxed puckering to the surface like a hungry fish, and artful fingers can handle the glass sliver so deftly that the heart must swallow it like a pill? Delta Tells has instructed me in all this herself. So how does she know?"

His questions waited upon no answer. They dredged deeper the channel of fears that ran through him then, floating larger and more buoyant imaginings of the wife's bloody capacity. Now he could begin to see how remarks dropped casually from the corner of her mouth, gestures released like birds into air, presentiments in a cloudy eye, while perfectly gnomic in themselves, enconstellated in the telescopic extension of his memory, a divinatory meaning.

Brainard Tells' speech suddenly surged with the momentum of lines connecting impatient dots as he pictured his wife for the first time, in the act of her words.

"I will make you a body that fills nothing more than the want of his own wife," she had said.

Perhaps in the dark, she had stood over him measuring him by the lengths of the longest kitchen knife, his sleeping bulk illuminated only by the lightning flashes of her tempestuous darting around the four corners of the bed. Was there a trunk in the house where she had tried her own size to anticipate the number of cuts she must make, in order to make him fit? Had she even fallen asleep there so to enhance the wakeful vividness of her most vengeful dream?

"I will show you how the body is its own prisoner, she had said, "howevermuch the husband complains of his wife's possessiveness, however freely he breaks from her embrace."

Perhaps she had even followed him at night when he lifted himself like the lightest coverlet from their bed. He always used the latest hour of the night like a ladder lowered into the street. He found the pitch of darkness more conducive to his longings than the light in which one sees the object in one's grasp, even before touching it. It always seemed that he had merely to reach out into an unfathomable depth of midnight and the blindest movements of his body made a pathway to another woman's embrace, where she might be waiting for him in a street that does not turn in any direction, waiting beneath a lamp whose light has been taken by a stone, waiting in a square whichcan be entered from different directions, waiting where assignation is only another thrust into the darkness.

How could Delta have followed him in such labyrinthine designs if she were not even darker in her own ways than he?

Had Delta followed him? Followed them?

Followed them down blind alleys? Followed them into an underground tunnel—railroad tracks running over their heads—their agile shadow, turned upon a single bodily axis against the seeping wall of the tunnel that curled wavelike above their heads? Had Delta, his shadow's own dog, stood close enough behind his undulant form to aid the upswing of the other woman's bared, white leg, as if she, his wife, were his own right arm? Had Delta actually stood behind him in the spasmodic instant when even the thought of who he was suddenly burst from itself, the muzzle of her gun held so tightly against his turned back that only the other woman—where she was pinned against the wall—might have felt the extra force as something more than feeling.

Then why had Delta forborne the trigger?

Had the idea of a more perfect revenge burst upon her consciousness in that moment of concussive silence? Had she sustained the instantaneous impact of the decision to act differently, like the shadow which falls before the body struck down on top of it?

Now Brainard Tells could believe that he had himself been there at the moment of conception and so father to the deed she conceived against himself. But only now, in the heated distensions of memory, did the idea of the crime reach the full gestation of the image that thwarted him: she pierced the child through a starry blue quiltlet, blinding herself to the act in order to accomplish it more effortlessly. She had plunged the knife through a downy blue firmamentto penetrate the flesh of Brainard's own earth-weighted body.

At last he *saw* what she had been talking about: the aproned mother, poised breathlessly in her kitchen, the small bundle barely stirring on the counter under her open palm. In the other hand, the knife had already become the cold mirror of her averted gaze, as if she had slipped from the world into the glass by which she contemplated her presence in it. Then the motion—swift, certain—from which all thinking is fled, as when she who would be miraculously healed throws the crutches out from under eager, extended, empty, arms.

"From that moment it would have been only a matter of following the recipe. The numbered steps would have become a steep staircase against which she would have had to steady her hand and her eye, gaining the equilibrium necessary to proceed.

"Perhaps, in the commotion of crockery taken down from the shelf, she imagined she had simply lost the child to a convivial crowd of friends and relations. She might easily return to them, as the hostess to her party. So in the activity of ranking bowls of different sizes, arranging implements on the counter, selecting ingredients from the shelves, even sopping the wet surfaces which would have to be cleared for the further sorting of parts, there would have been a solacing order: as when one closes the door against the crowded room of the party. Then one counts the doorways along the lengthening hallway as rapturous increments of silence, until the ears are plugged, the eyes are blurred by the light which beckons from the other end of the tunnel. A subtle quickening of the pace lifts the weight from one's feet."

In the silence that grew around these last words, the listeners wondered that Brainard Tells had talked himself to sleep. So deeply had his head sunk into the white pillow it would not have been more incredible if he had been taken up into a cloud.

Those who heard it with their own ears felt the story come to roost in another part of their bodies. What had fluttered in their ribcages, although their chairs had not moved, suddenly alighted with the unsettling weight of an egg descending into the pelvic nest.

"Delta tells lies," she said, who had lifted herself to sweep the nervous, beaded dampness from her seat.

"Delta Tells says the child is with his father, wherever he is. And she is smiling with her mouth open for me to count the teeth.

"She says 'Homunculus' is the name of the dish she prepares.

"'The recipe is every woman's dowry.' She calls herself a traditional woman. Her husband was her first man, she says, and the child is her last. She should know. By the hand that now covers her mouth—whether to quell a horror or to cover a giggle—she has delivered us of our own children.

"Her hand to my womb too has coaxed the sounds of life. Lying in Delta's charge, feeling the membraneous pronouncement about to burst from my stuttering groin, I saw only Delta's head pincered between my thighs.

"'Make it speak,' she urged. And the softest movement of her mouth disgorged what my own thigh muscles, stiffened to iron pokers, could not pry loose.

"But, practically turning a dancestep close to the bed post and with the still unswaddled birth echoing in her swaying arms, she told me that I had lost my tongue, and would never speak from that region of my body again.

"Now I am a mother of eight, and Delta's words could not be heard over the swell of their laughter."

"Delta tells lies," she said, who wriggled against the stiffness of the chairback as if she were releasing a snake from her spine.

"Delta Tells says that the woman's own womb makes a perfect echo chamber for the cries of her man.

"'She eats him up, doesn't she?' she said, drawing the words with a pronounced suction of her lips.

"I will not be drawn in. Yet I confess, I have let her draw me out.

"Once she said she would show me the shape of my own ovaries, each as ready as a raspberry on its prickly stem. By putting one hand inside me and taking my own in her other—as softly as one leads a child to bed—she made me follow the innermost track of my self, where so she promised, I would discover, and for the first time, the meaning of 'mine'.

"I must lie flat, she ordered. I must spread my hand like a soft cloth over my midriff. Only my head was propped high enough to see where she—in the tremulous V of my canted legs— had entered, still looking back at me, but gone behind the eyes. She worked her invisible hand from the marionette lift and plunge of the visible shoulder. Then, beneath the magician's cape of my own spread fingers she turned me inside out. Through her most recondite touch I felt myself emerge in the palpated braille of her manipulations.

"'This is the tip of my finger,' Delta said, pressing as though it were the stylus of the pen itself drawing upon the interior of my abdomen the shapes of organs that concatenated against one another like images jostling in a mirror held up to another mirrory surface, shuddering echoes of the push she gave them with her prodding finger. Those watery undulations rose up like a vision of the kindest face to the peaceful surface of my belly, where I had dropped my eyes, where I picked at the surface of that mirror. Then, atop the protruding stiffneck by which I recognized that most recessed sensation of Delta's insistent finger poking me from within, I felt a tiny head, bobbling, hard, crenulated brain shape. It was variegated beyond any capacity for sensation known to my own squeamish fingertips, between which—as she told me then—the hive of life was buzzing to be born!

"But the echoing rooms of my home are yet vacant

of children's laughter, and since the moment that I released what I held then, in a motion so much like casting a fiery seed into a moist furrow, I have been unable to keep a grip on anything smaller than the tips of my fingers."

"Delta tells lies," she said, who stood up so brusquely the chair might have come out of her.

"Delta Tells says that the body of the woman is not her own any more than the man who calls her his. But she would give me mine, she bargained, if I would give her my credulous mind.

"She said she was the woman wronged, whom all have heard tell of. If I would tell it too, she would find a way to nestle the egg so warmly, so deeply within me that it must certainly hatch from my shivering pelvis.

"She would show me how to make my Olaf move in the darkness so that every crooked corner of the way would melt into an oceanic medium for his swimming self.

"Her fingers would lead the way. 'A woman must lie back to find out what she really feels,' Delta said, and pressed upon my forehead to indicate the position.

"I watched her hand alight from my own forehead, fall beneath my waist. Just as anything which the eye has frozen in its most contemplative stare dissolves into some more supple medium of sensation, so Delta's hand became the feeling of my own self, flooding the way of her entry, floating her words of sober instruction.

"'Make this Olaf mount you only after he has built a mound of pillows high enough to give you buoyancy. But let him think of himself as the swimmer, so that he might find a wriggle in his being—though it makes you giggle—to loosen all the knots of distance between you. In fact, the deeper the laughter, the stronger the swimmer's exertions against the abysmal pull of the bottom.

"'When he finds the crest of that motion and you hear the spray of foam in his nostrils, let the uplifted weight of him fall through you like a net. Let it make a taut plumb line through all your murky depth to the place where I am holding you now.

"'By the tips of my fingers, I have what you want most from yourself.'

"When, an instant later, she snapped the very fingers before my eyes to show me how simple was the task, she must have pulverized the finest grain of my being between them. For though she gave me my sons, they bear not the faintest imprint of my own features. Rather, the cleft forehead, the pulpy snout, the drizzled chin, and the black seeded eyes of Olaf are what I behold in the smudged mirror of my womb."

Delta Tells refused to speak more of the child's disappearance. To the three inquisitors who presented themselves on her doorstep she averred the child's whereabouts were no more mysterious to her than the absence of credulity which had attended her own now faded words of contrition.

"I have confessed already." She made them feel that even now the child hovered in her words, a wraith visible only in the trajectory of her pointing finger. "What I said then is buried in your own hearing. It remains for you to excavate that sound if you wish to know what kind of bone it might be for you to chew on."

Yet she did not close the door. She stood more portentously in the space as if it were meant to hold her. If she would neither step aside nor shut the door, this was because she wanted them to think of her as a picture in a frame, to wonder whose lost daughter she herself might prove to be. What loving fingers had pressed the white edges of the picture into the green embrace of the felt backer? Whose loving heart had pulsed with the lullabye of longing that was now audible in the tapping of Delta's foot upon the threshold, pointing up the distance in time as well as space that separated the three inquisitors from their answer.

When suddenly she did step toward them, the visitors could only believe she was at last surrendering to the sense of touch, if only to the conviviality of the shaking hand. By embracing her in that manner, they might at least gain some ballast against the rising bubble of her scornful speech.

She took three steps before she struck the first of the three men dead in the fork of his trousers. But it was not a blow so much as a grip, seeking something like the poise that balances the bright beam of cutlery on a tense fulcrum of thumb and two fingers, *not* raising it to the ready lip. Nor did the victim appear to be able to move, except to tighten the pursestrings of his mouth, the lips bunching over the teeth that stained through them.

And no one touched Delta Tells.

For the Superintendent of Mines, who could only spread his legs farther apart—rather than clench a stance that might be levered into tender footsteps—the two fingers dampening his inseam seemed to press hardest upon the glottal stop at the base of his throat. They held his tongue to the roof of his mouth, sent a misty gurgle into his sinuses. It might have been his head in her hand which would certainly shatter if she dropped it now.

Then her wrist began to turn. The small bones in her wrist were the vivisectionist's pins pricking the most minute details of this specimen's splayed sensations.

No one else spoke. The words of the two companions might have been wriggling on the shaft of the same pin by which she held the Superintendent in place. And nothing moved outside the orbit described by the turning of her wrist, though a subtly global circumference throbbed on its axis.

He, pregnant with a sensation that seemed to arise outside his body, could only wait for the spell of gravity to be broken. His mind was held in awe, as if by the motion of heavenly bodies that are observable only by the light that is lost between them.

"Here you are," Delta broke the silence, though her grip remained firm, the circular motion of her hand remained constant.

"You were undiscovered to yourself. So what was not missing is found. Child's play, is it not? So is it not what you were looking for after all?"

Then she drew away her hand, so that he could see what felt merely leaden between his legs, though it had made the loose material of his trousers fly up: a black wingflap, broken in midflight, frozen against a melting sky.

His eyes had flown into the top of his head on the same wings.

As if out of the same sky, the eyes of his two companions fell upon him then. And because the woman stood well apart from him now, the Superintendent of Mines could only behold his glaring erection as something to be seen beyond any power of thought or action. When he bowed his head to look at himself, there was no mistake that the accusatory finger pointed at him.

Because what covered him revealed him, there was no recourse to a further fig leaf. And because what stood out so clearly against the membraneous weave of his clothing was thereby in its grip, any turning of his body away from view was bound to rouse the ghost of the caress that had mothered his humiliation, though Delta's hand was suddenly the blur of a fist in his vision, she shook it so violently in his stricken face.

"Now you may not ask ever again after any child of mine, nor think what comes into a woman's mind from the body of a man. Now something has happened to you which will make you think what can occur in a body that cannot be held by the mind. Here is the flesh of your flesh!"

Again her hand swung out. But this time the lightest touch she was capable of produced nothing so much as the swaying of the cradle in the tensile heft of his trousers, if ever a cradle was rocked with such vehemence.

She closed the door behind her.

Brainard Tells lay with his tongue heavy on his mind: tumescent, jellied mass, rooted in the cellar of his voice. Brainard weighed its knowledge against his most profound contemplation of what had happened.

Something his tongue had tasted would be the answer to his question. And, like some fat and glistening larval stage of intuition, it seemed to fill his mouth with expectation. But he would have to touch it to make it move.

Delta had once guided him with one rough finger to find the separate places of sweet and sour, salt and bitter, the whole tongue's skin alive like a prickling rash with the ingrown bristles of sensation. Now he would need memory to take him back. It had tasted something sweet and salty, sour and bitter. So the whole organ would be of use to him in his search.

Though now it lolled between the rows of teeth, he would prod it, so he thought to himself, from within, from a single salivating corpuscle of remembered salubriousness that would stiffen the wet muscle into an arching, leaping, splashing sea life, breaking the grey surface of his bewilderment. And from the sheer physical duration of that spasm he would milk the strength of memory, would gather the sparkling instant of expired sensation into the longer reaches of time that he needed to guess what artful confection of meat and sauce he had tasted that might have so emboldened his own wife to declare that he had eaten his own!

But though his tongue would tell, he knew he must first be led by the nose. The tongue pulled from the inside. The nose went out. And he was bound to see things inside out. This is what Delta had already taught him, he believed, by her penchant for saying one thing in place of another. Riddling. To know this, he thought, was already part of the solution.

"You have eaten your own." The words were a false scent. Instead he would follow the trail of grease-heaving smoke that led to the encampment of gypsy stoves sprawled beyond the last boundary of paved streets. There the smells of cooking would possess their candor as the bone claims its meat. Every sultry spore that passed his nostrils would excite his sensitivity, develop his capacity to distinguish, help him to choose the flavor of his dead reckoning.

Where else but among gypsy smells would his wife have discovered the ruse of dressing plainest rabbit or squirrel in a spicy cloak, an aromatic veil, a coat of such syrupy richness that the eater wouldn't think to question what was underneath until it was already sewn into the tightening seams of his aching gut?

So Brainard Tells realized that this time he would be foraging for sauce.

He would delve among gypsy secrets for his answer. And the dark-eyed, full-breasted women dripping over their seething pots would be happy to have a man at the stoves, lifting the pot lids, giving a stir to whatever simmers or boils, daubing his fingers, tasting, nodding, smacking his lips. It would be the sauce of his own disguise to flatter their ingredients.

Then his tongue would do double duty. A stroking word would elicit a touch to the quivering bud, a tickle, a taste. He would have to taste every sauce to savor the one that still clutched at the bottom of his throat. Then his tongue might be like the hand of rescue reaching over the whistling cliff edge, a savior to his memory.

For when he had doused himself in the right pot, he would finally be able to shake off the spell of his wife's too well-prepared words. Then he would know exactly what it was that could be pressed from a fruity pulp, crushed from an oily bean, or sweated from the skin of a chicken, to cause even the most sobering gut to belch the credulity of the thought that tastes like a child.

Only the jut of tongue would be left to ponder what it had shoved toward oblivion. The mind evaporates in that thought.

"You have eaten your own!"

He realized that the cook would have possessed extraordinary powers to savvy the flavor that went with that idea. It called of course for the feat of making one taste swallow another, a palatable confusion of the thing remembered with what it was not, a dish which knows no bottom of the pot.

So, if he wanted a word from the cook, Brainard Tells would have to look for a face that was a mask of its own nature. She would be the keeper of the kettle in which he felt himself coming to a boil. If he looked only for what was not apparent, he would know her to be the one in whom his wife had seen what she wanted.

So, sight, smell, and taste would be the order of his senses.

And then, should memory serve him well, the sweating knot of uncertainty that bulked inside his shallow chest might soften into the regular pulse of understanding, spreading inside him like the bodily ease that can only be taken after a great exertion.

He would even be flattered to share a witching knowledge of how the clearest broth can be thickened—by spice alone—to strike the human tongue with a thought so visceral that it might have licked its own brain.

"*Work ceases in the mine when no one knows what to think.*

"*Something has hatched out from a goggle-eyed inspector's brittle question—'What about eggs?'—that brings the second shift up early. Then each man's questioning brain becomes the ringing awareness of an empty interior.*

"*Entrances are sealed off. Generators are halted. Air vents desist from their heavy respiration. The workers are ordered home to sit by their phones.*

"*But a foreman who lets a few portentously rounded words extrude from his officially tight lips draws enough curiosity seekers—despite the chill drizzle—to warm the nest of rumor around the echoing hole.*

"*But no man knows what to think.*

"*For two days they only know that the men who*

operate the elevator, big enough for a cargo of elephants, are not miners. And the unassuming workers who are permitted to descend into the mine with anthill efficiency, are delivered to the job each morning in compact black cars bearing stencilled white numbers on the door panels. And their only speech is a mouthful of numbers echoing out of the shaft in the crackling signals of a badly tuned radio frequency.

"A stark white light shines like splintered bone out of the ground at the hour when the night shift would have ordinarily been lowered into a mote of visible darkness.

"Nothing anthricite is passed out under the eyes of the watchers, who finally dwindle away behind their own front doors to endure the waiting. But wooden crates go in. Unassembled, they do not auger the shapes of what it is speculated they might hold.

"Only the mouth of rumor fills up with anything that gives substance to the waiting. Otherwise the men experience their idleness as a gradual lightening. And feeling airy as they do with the empty atmosphere of these impatient days ,they almost fear being carried off like the balloon slipped from a child's hand.

"With such thoughts swelling imagination, they wait helplessly for that other punctual burst of air, the steam whistle, which might at last mark a time to set their feet against the rotation of the earth again, to regain the gravitational force of a work routine that bellies into the orbit of the sun.

"On the seventh day the miners are called to work, but not in the usual way. The word goes from house to house as the announcement of a wedding or a death. Because the word is only in the air no single man can feel confident that he has really been called.

"But falling in together on the steep slate sidewalk that leads to the plant entrance ,they strengthen the feeling, stiffen their legs into a marching gait. So they appear in an almost regimental order before the fortress-like rampart of the number one shaft. A double shift of men stand side by side who are otherwise separated from one another by nothing less than the sun and the moon, around which they can reach their hands only through the most extenuating labors of the shovel and the pick.

"None of the men, pressing forward against the bars of the gate when they hear clangorous cables begin to tighten against the counterweight of a cold, grey, steel floor that would accommodate at least fifty men, see the phalanx of women rising on the road against their backs. Nor do they hear the calling voices.

"Though the lilting sounds come from behind, the accompaniment of this sound to the sight of the massive elevator chassis, ascending into view, mating with its skeletal housing, its naked girders, creates at the moment of contact the impression of a strange tuning fork in the air, clasping everything and everyone together into a single, solemn beat of anticipation.

"The women have been invited by the mine management. Though it has been an afterthought, it is not one that can even begin to penetrate the heads of their husbands, brothers and fathers who wonder too tumultuously for words how so many women could appear behind their backs, so inexplicably, even before the workers' own reasons for being present might receive confirmation in that mystical expansion of air which is the foreman's voice straining through a plastic bullhorn. The men's hands are already enfolded in the hands of their women before they can speak of the mysterious ways of such communion.

"Then the iron gates chime open. Another beat of the measure for which their feet have not yet found the rhyming dancestep.

"But no one needs to be told what to do. They proceed, almost all in couples now, all of them stepping aboard the shaft elevator, ready to be lowered to the fullest depth. They are ready to swallow leagues of darkness. They are shoulder to shoulder and closer than ever for the overcrowding of the steel carriage in which they will feel the descent through their feet.

"'The greater the weight, the greater the vibration.'

"But this is a saying that the men will never again be able to impart to their wives in the manner of the storyteller casting off to exotic shores. Because now they all weigh together in the same body of knowledge. They all lose their stomachs to the same sensation of plummet. They are all jolted together—at the moment of their landing—into a recognition

*that they have indeed caught the beat for which their fright-
ened embrace of one with another is now revealed to be the urge
of an irresistible but unimaginable dance.*

*"Only after he has begun to speak are the paired
companions aware of the only solitary figure who has accompanied their descent. In its shocking presence, the mammoth
voice is indistinguishable from the excesses of absorbent white
light that suddenly takes them off their bearings like the spell
of invisibility from which no amount of the audience's incredulous blinking can summon back the magician's beautiful
assistant.*

*"The man's voice—he might as well be a magician—
is the ghost of all their vanished bodies, as they reach out,
grasping in blindness for another realm of sensation to prop
against.*

*"The first ones to be brought back to their physical
selves are the ones who stumble painfully against the searing
cast iron housings of several enormous arc lights strategically
arranged on the uneven floor of the shaft to focus all attention
in a direction that few of them have yet dilated sufficiently to
see.*

*"The man's voice is an excited crackle of electricity
that burns through the cloud of confusion billowing beneath
their uplifted arms, their floating faces. And then, as if the two
phenomena are connected by something as tensile with gal-
vanic energy as a wire, the eyes, adjusting to the stunning glare
in rounder and rounder proportions of amazement, become the
opening through which the man's words instantly communi-
cate with the seers, not the sounds, but the sight—tunnelling
through to them—of what has been freshly excavated at their
feet. They stand together on a precipice though there is no
appreciable drop below them. Instead, a shallow trench yawns
away from their feet like a receding wave, exposing what at
first appears only to be the toothmarks of whatever hydraulic
jaws, gone wildly out of the control of the operator's hands,
have bitten ferociously into the obsidian wall of the shaft.*

*"'Thtegathauruth,'" he proclaims. The word is like an
ivory tusk cutting through his protruded lip because, as loud as
his voice is, the lisp comes through that much stronger.*

"And now, because in the softening glare of the light

they can see the speaker shrunken beside his voice, he seems that much smaller than the thing he gestures toward. But the excitement flexing in his shoulder blades like aboriginal wings straining through the taut material of a suit jacket—somehow cut too small even for this hummingbird of a man—makes it seem that he will momentarily be twittering above it.

"And the voice shines brighter in the words that name each jagged puzzle piece of horn and bone, tooth and claw, so that the viewer's eye, bulked with recognition of what gradually takes shape before it, might turn to stone itself in the bulging intensity of that gaze.

"Then the amplifying sibilance of the lisp, thick as a tungsten filament in the aura of what it illuminates, scratches more fiercely at the eardrum, as if to further unearth the faculty of sight itself from its embeddedness in the voice of instruction:

"'The name of thith bone ith medeacolchith.'

"A horn worthy of a rhinoceros impales sight. It is the only bone that does not bear the imprint of whatever larger beast has crumpled the rest of the skeleton now shockingly spread out before the viewers' eyes. The bone, for all its sharpness, was no defense against what has obviously crushed the animal from behind, scattering the whole bodily structure into a pattern that might be mistaken for the shards of its broken teeth. They are arrayed in pieces small enough, but over an area too wide for even the most monstrous jaws.

"'Thith reptile, rethembling a rhinotheroth, but of a thize large enough to carry a thecond thelf within itth mammoth girth, lived over theven million yearth ago, in a yawning exthpanth of time and thpathe!'

"There is so little distance between the tongue and the ear in the force of this revelation that the listeners—only just become seers—experience the clarity of the moment as a membranous tremor through which sight resonates back into sound and with such a palpable quaver of excitement that touch seems to become its medium.

"Between each of the tottering partners—thrown off balance again by this reversal of senses—touch is the fulcrum of their struggle to retain the balance of four legs. Upon the tilting axis of such longing they slide into one another's arms to kiss.

"*Lips wet with the ferverence of probing tongues, ears stoppered with echoing sibilance, eyes blocked with light, they taste what could not be otherwise experienced for the sensation that leaves no room for any other sense.*

"*And in that embrace there is a crushing of bones too, masticating the perseverant voice where it charts a path from the polestar horn, along the spinal ridge to the stuttering ellipses of bright neck bones, everything—especially the skull, indistinguishable from the smallest tail bone—impacted now in the same proximity of enconstellation.*

"*But the human sounds of kissing thicken against even the swell of the voice that will not desist from its staccato enumeration of the bone fragments splintering infinitesimally into the stark polysyllablism of their names. If anyone has eyes to see the flecks scintillating upon flecks of fossil luminescence, they seem to be bursting from the eons-cooled rock like a shadow of the million showering sparks had first laid the molten darkness over them.*

"*Instead a hand that moves invisibly through the excesses of blaring, revelatory light pulls every man and woman into a pit of darkness, with what any of them can only imagine must be the long, levered arm of the electric circuit box. For all its necessary bulk and pitch-black contrast, no one recalls it from their glaring memory of the illuminated space where it stood out so sharply only moments before.*

"*Total darkness. Then the sounds of kissing thicken the darkness into a syrupy slowness which the spokesman's lonesome voice stumbles upon as if into a vast tar pit. The last syllables will never be extracted from the last word where utterance is stuck.*

"*And then the articulating cadences of Latinate speech are replaced with a sound of bodily motion, sweating out a more astringent intensity of darkness. The flexing ligature of this dark body is a rising temperature in the cavernous dark, intimating in its pulse the flow of rocky substances. A labored breathing bubbles through the flow, a weightless tumescence fills the lungs. So many sucking mouths hung from the nippled darkness. Closeness fits into the palm of a mastering, moistening hand in which everything is held together. What can only be piles of discarded clothing echo the absorption of*

*bodily weight that sounds through toneless waves of muscular
heat. Bones moving in the aura of flesh attain the lightness of
expanding air. The darkness inflates as well, warmed by the
massive haunches of some newly roused emotion, lifting an
expulsion of low moans upon its thrashing back though the
moaning seems to echo from a groveling belly.*

*"Heaving the weight of that belly in which the fermen-
tation of darkness is at its pitch of effervescence, the groans
and urgent bleats of the tiny, sleek head that is undoubtedly
craning somewhere above, exerts a pull upon all disproportionate weight below that snap the cord of life between them but
is instead the fulcrum of coordination upon which intimations
of a long-necked behemoth suddenly lumber into physical
space like the breath of any heavy object falling past your
face."*

"And that is what I told you?" was Brainard Tells'
reply.

To the white smocked attendant, the egg-shaped
impression sunk in the pillow beneath the patient's raised
head could have been the mark of a violent fist, for all the
fury that stood out on the inquiring face. The patient
would not lie back. Nor would he let the question drop
from between his teeth though he shook it as listlessly as
the shredded rag in the mouth of a tired dog.

"I did not tell it in your words, but it was as you
dreamt it to me, if you were dreaming," the attendant
explained.

And then he masked his effort to restrain the
patient's agitation with the gesture of a hand soliciting a
feverish forehead.

But the attendant's open palm, stung as hotly as if
he had struck the patient across a blue cheek. The patient

pushed his face upward through the depth of his incredulity. He was a man struggling to breathe through a fathom of clear water which holds the sky deceptively out of reach. Though his eyes are filled with it, he cannot take a breath. The words seemed to collapse his windpipe in incremental deflations of his will to speak.

"Neither my words nor my meaning," was all he could expel. Yet his hands were still free enough to tear away the mask which, for Brainard Tells, only *appeared* to be the startled face of the white-smocked orderly.

Hours later, when Brainard Tells awoke to the thought of the needle prick that had syphoned off his consciousness, his questions were more sedate: "And I have only been lying here, in this infirmary bed? And the child is still missing? And the woman who is still my wife will not speak of what she has done?"

His questions were the fingers modelling his own brain matter if he held it in the grip of impatient hands.

Delta Tells lost her thumbs in the medium of malleability. Sitting stiffly against the same chairback that would have hugged her husband's stomach to the table edge at supper time, she let the eight fingers of both hands extend across the curvature of the orb that was so subtly beginning to pulsate in her lap. Wings folded over a warming egg, her hands fluttered to keep it warm. The warmer the softer was a rule of thumb. Then she could have touched thumbs, they probed so closely to one another at the softening center.

With the leverage of both thumbs against the flexing palms of her hands, she began to knead the wax, letting it extrude from the rolled palms, gathering it up again on her fingertips, working it into a perspirational languor. Through the warmth radiating back into her body from the softening of the wax, she thought of her fingertips as faintly pollinated with the flavor of the honey. Such thoughts, she was thinking, were to the cells of the honeycomb what the flavor of the honey was to the smell of the flowers from which the bees had first sucked it. Memory was impressed upon the wax before it ever received the first imprint of a human craving.

Delta herself could not forget that the wax weighing in her hands now—though it was probably equal to the weight of the brain pressing such awareness against her forehead with a painful throb of recognition—had once fit into the pit of a child's palm. It was a ball for the first time in *her* grip. Her father who had scooped it from the hive like pulp from a fruit rind had had to scrape his hand across her own to make it come off in a lumpish smear.

And with that, a buzzing had descended over her thoughts, gathering about her ears as much symmetry as the wax rolled up into a perfect orb between the heated, circular motions of her rubbing hands. So round as it was, she could not resist the urge to flatten it.

And there, minted for the first time on the face of the tiny waxen disc, she recognized the intersecting lines which drew her fate. This coinage would be the currency of her will where it drew her upon the pathway of her intricately branching lifeline, indelible mark of her own impressionability in the wax. It cleft the hollows of her palm when she held it up to her view like a mirror. Her father instructed her that the wax was better than a glass for looking at such things.

Her father had showed her how the impression one left upon the wax was something to be felt more than seen. The face in the mirror is water, by comparison. By comparison, the whorling thumbprint trods upon the wax to feel the turning of the earth within its stride. The mirror-image washes away under the tidal comings and goings of supplicant eyes. But if the thumb pushes belligerently into its own imprint, though it smears the identifying mark, it sustains an expansion. In the mirror the objects lie flat, planar, oblique to one another, exposing sharp edges, precipices. But in the soft malleability of the wax, all sharp edges succumb to the globular shape that is their deeper nature.

Because at first the ball of wax was no bigger than a prize marble, Delta Tells started with tiny objects.

The first step through the looking glass always imprinted the heel of her open palm. Within the artful frame of that impression she would be able to fit the smallest parts of her body: a fingernail, a knuckle, two teeth, one eye closed, her navel.

But because the hives were ceaselessly buzzing with their secretions, it was not long before Delta was able to ball up into the size of a fist what the closed fist had at first easily contained.

As it grew, the ball of wax gathered fresh sensations and the hardness of their sedimentation began to sink in: a fish hook, a thimble, a key, a finger, a bird's beak, a cat's paw, a doll's face, a chicken bone, a comb, a teaspoon, a belt buckle, a string of beads, a knife blade, a heart-shaped medallion, a pill box, a fountain pen, a nail file, a smile, a cigarette holder, an ermine claw, a bullet, a bra clasp, a bronze shoe, a mason jar, a railroad spike, a dog's skull, a curling iron, an axehead.

The greater the mass of the wax over time, the harder it became to soften it up. The more impressions were convolvulated within its membranous warmth, the stronger the ache in the hands that squeezed and worked the wax. For every shape preserved within the growing circumference of the ball of wax, the shaping hands contorted to encompass new dimensions of their labor.

Only one impression had ever broken the mold of such elastic substance. Once, crouching naked, balancing on the balls of her feet in a shadowy corner of her bedroom, and with her hands thrust deeply between her parted legs, Delta shifted her center of gravity forward onto the curving surface of what she held between them. Mounted so upon the pommel of her design, letting the weight of her whole being settle into cupped hands, she waited for the warmth of her body to breathe life into the waxen form. But, when she pressed the wax template of that kiss to the breathy speechlessness of her puckering mouth, the heat-thinned medium ruptured as if a torrent of harsh words had passed through the parted lips.

What she balled up into the tightest fist she could make at that moment contained only the breath of motion that chases a fly from the hand that would have grasped it. Now, years afterward and even in the accretion of three times the size of her girlish fist, the hollowness of that gesture still throbbed at the center of the enveloping wax.

Now, though the ball of wax was in her lap, it pleased her to think of it as the size of a man's head. Weighing so, it evoked the braided torsion of the neck—tendons standing in relief like engorged blood vessels—from which it would have been dependent if it were a heavy head. And as obdurate as the waxen head was to the touch, it helped her to think of her fingers in her husband's hair as clutching the roots of his thought.

Where thought yielded to the touch, Delta's hands would always be busy, pressing, smoothing, twisting, squeezing, stretching, kneading, emitting through their effacement of all the engraved images resident within the wax the shapes of their own industriousness like unconscious thoughts, the grip of a larger, more encompassing hand, the massage of another message.

Now that her hands were warmed to her work, she felt a glow of reciprocity dawn from the slipperiness they induced. The easier the motion, the more thoughtless her movements, though such thoughtlessness became more and more the intimation of her husband's head as she would have liked to know it best: her fingers fitted to the furrows of his brain would feel them as extrusions of the flexion housed inside each knuckle like a snail in its shell. Their cracking would give her access to an inwardness which the smoothness of the physical motion belied with its quickening accretions of slipperiness.

In such sensations, inside and outside met like the face in the mirror. Every thumb-thrust and palm-squeeze liquified with the increasing malleability of the medium from which new shapes were constantly emerging. These slippery extrusions were ideas she had never had about her husband's mind. Their firmness was matched by their newness, the one state connected to the other by the transformations that wrought one from another in a deepening convulsion of elasticity.

By now she had worked the wax long enough that if she pulled the labile mass in two directions, it would have stretched wider than her arms could reach away from her body, if she were in full flight. But the weight was still vibrant enough, if she bounced it against her open palms, to remind her how it cast the shadow of her husband's head and how the thoughts that it held, however winged with evanescence, would follow the arc of gravity if she had anything to do with it.

So, now, with her hands opened flat in her lap and the wax weighing upon her consciousness of them there— with expectancy brightening her face—she began to bend to it as if over the surface of a still pool to see what she could see.

The crack of vertebrae was the sound she heard when her face hit the surface of what, out of all the fervent handling—and because she had *not* pulled it apart—she had unconsciously modelled into the shape of an impatient egg. She had only intended an oval, broad and plump enough to frame the features of her face. Now, because she could not breathe, she knew it held them all: slivered almond eyes, porcelain cheekbones, large petaled lips and—struggling most in the suffocating grip of that life-mask—the perfectly aquiline nose, which in her father's mind remained the most faithful memorial of her mother's frail beauty.

Now plugged with the wide aroma of a sweetly sucked meadow—she was inhaling after all—her own nose led her to the impression that was most deeply embedded in the honeyed wax:

Because she was the bee-keeper's daughter, because she could not think of her father without mentally parting the nets that draped the brim of his straw hat, she had always associated the malleability of the wax with the incessant gyrations of the corkscrew stinger. Motion was the meaning of both of them. But in her memory the stinger came first.

Before she could take the honey, beaded up and glistening on the flat stick her father played upon her lips, he made her sit at a low wooden table. He made her peer through a magnifying lens that crouched on four bent metal legs, like the more predatory bug, above the specimen he had collected. In the golden viscosity of the lens the bee was restrained in a gossamer harness fashioned of the same mesh that screened her father's eyes. Its legs moved as through a watery current that drew it backwards. Then, into the slow convexity of that glass an invisible hand introduced a long needle, shining and pronged so as to mate movectly with the spurred anatomy of the insect, which it now clasped in a fit of convulsive stillness, and exposed more nakedly to her view. First the stinger. Then the salubrious taste of the honey.

How else would she have come to the idea that by flexing one's tongue in the darting sunlight, it would be possible to milk the bee of its most delicious nectar through the very point that pierces?

She knew well how the buzzing insects flew to buds when they opened. So with her lips quite far apart, with her tongue stretched taut enough to make the buds bristle at its tip, she waited amidst the towering bee boxes—and so out of her father's sight—for the first touch of taste.

But it was a vibration of air, a tuft of frenetic motion which drew her own eyes to the tip of her nose and made her intensely aware of it as the blind spot which concealed the most tensile extremity of her tongue. She knew it was no motion of the sun that had made her tongue the shadow of her nose. Rather it was the shape of her head—suddenly sharper in her mind's eye than ever before—that etched this lucidity. And a triangulating line of sight that followed the straining convexity of one eyeball to the tip of her tongue—because it had to pierce her nose—drew her out a diagrammatic distance from herself to see so clearly the image of what now most urgently buzzed within her brain: the profile of a pink and blond, pigtailed child balancing a bee—black as a storm cloud, poised as explosively as a burst of pollen—on the furthest reach of her tongue.

Drawn out to such a fine point, the tongue might have pierced its purpose.

Instead it licked the orb of wing-beaten air and in the

gravitational pull of that mirror-smooth motion it caught the barb as a wave of blown silk catches the nail on the wall. The lightning prick was indistinguishable from that reflex of the tongue which snatched the bee into the hovering darkness of her closed mouth.

Then her most livid pain was the muscle that locked her jaws against the bee's escape. The involuntary fierceness of her own bite imprisoned the scream that beat scaly wings inside her head and swelled its breast against the features of surprise heaving all over her face. She felt her head could burst from itself: finally, the face husked from its shadows, the egg hatched from its shell.

But the stinger was still in her, implanted even more deeply because she could not open her mouth. And her mouth had become so small in proportion to the pain that lurched within it, that all freedom of movement seemed to be lost among its parts. She felt her larynx chafing against the ribs of her palate. Her uvula seeped like a hot tear from that puckering duct which was all the opening of her soundless throat. She was forced to stretch her neck in an awkward gulleting motion to keep her tonsils free of the involuntary chattering of the back molars and from the snapping tension of the jaw muscles against which the bones still struggled to pry open her lips.

Though it was all inside her, everything tightening around the engorgement of her tongue brought into fine and tactile relief the two polyhedronal domed eyes, the wings like overlapping shields, the brittle embrace of the six legs and manic flex of the thorax—attached like the thread to the cloth—where the bee had become the cruel intaglio of her enveloping flesh.

Ever more deeply incised in the soft medium of this pain, she felt the hardness of the alien body being swallowed beyond any capacity to spit. Regurgitation turned in upon itself like the inertia gathered within the pit of the stone when it has rolled to the very bottom of the hill.

Unmasking herself with a brittle snap of the neck, Delta Tells was surprised to see how the impression cast back at her from the shining declivities of the wax mold—which looked up at her from open palms—frowned upon the thought she cradled in her head. If she had filled the mold with wet plaster, the chill of recognition would not have hardened more stiffly than the word that was then shucked from her throat: "Honeylamb."

*****

Having submitted to the point of the stinger Delta Tells spread the salve of her sweetest memory.

She saw her father perspiring in a glow of concentration that was lighted by the frenzy of his own working hands. The flashes of steel that seemed to ignite from his fingertips illumined the press of his large thumbs against the dull edge of the razor blade (one in each hand) which was the slashing secret of his artistry. The strokes, as fine as hairs, showered the table top with wax shavings.

The translucence of the stroke revealed—as through a waxed casement—the shape of the head that shimmered in the shapeless mass. Though mountainously heaped, the substance of it would have smeared between two fingertips, the trove of the hive was so fresh from the multitudinous coveting of the bees. Softening, but not melting under the rays of such focused activity, it nonetheless supported the whittling hand of the gifted artisan whom Delta now knew her father to be. And with each pass of the hands over the slicker and slicker surface of this worked matter, the reflecting facets struck off by the flat of the steel blades fitted themselves as closely as finely- cut tesserae into a mosaic of vibrant light effects. Despite their planar provenance they curved into a dimension of roundness that coaxed the viewer off balance.

Falling, she caught the better sense of where she had been.

Father and daughter sat at oblique angles from one another. And between the artist's eye which moved like the imping thumb of perspective over the daughter's face, and the unraveling line of sight which the daughter cast back like an entanglement over the thing he modeled with his hands, there was a brittle refraction. Though the artist's concentration had sifted among the features of the daughter's face, he had composed the face of the mother's beauty on the table between them.

In this sculptural pronouncement Delta Tells recognized the features she had become acquainted with through the motions of her own face in the mirror, nodding to the insistence of her father's manipulating hand at her swayable chin. He told her that she carried the resemblance to her mother in the separate features of her face as if in separate compartments. Fluttering her face before the mirror, he was able to find, in the blur of those features, the focus of his nostalgia.

So, what had been made visible to her then, through a trick of motion, was stilled now into a feeling of certainty that did not solicit her incredulous touch. Now she was close enough to the face that had never shone for her—even in the wet depths of a photograph—that the daughter could not tell herself apart from the mother, in whose embrace she had never been so pressed. Nor could she pry her gaze apart from the form that met it. The sheen of the wax, warmed by the stroke of the shaving blades seemed to come out like an embarrassing sweat on the cheekbones, the inclining forehead, the smile for which the photograph would have been meant. Above all else, Delta recognized in the honey-colored eyes—though colorless against the hue of the head that held them in its sticky matrix—the color of her own hair, plaited and weighing against the back of her own head like the tail of a desert reptile smoldering upon a sun-baked rock.

Delta thought that the expression glistening upon that face might have radiated from a rock: giving back the kiss of sunlight through the unutterable chisel-mark that split the lips. The word in her father's mouth spit back at her from the sculpted head: *Honeylamb.*

Those who heard the story with their own ears slackened in the embrace of such a cruel account.

"Delta tells lies," she said, whose foot reached the floor with the shock of the whole body that has broken through thin ice.

"Delta Tells extols the gypsy physique. Delta Tells says the gypsy's stolid flesh holds its firm shape against the press of time as one's own husband can only in the flickering moment of his arousal. She says, women like us have the feel of it between thumb and forefinger and against the cuff of a curled palm. But, slick as it is with the salivations of desire, the engorgement we know in this manner resembles nothing so much as the snout of a dog rising to the scent of something hidebound in the air.

"But when I have pressed a coin into the gypsy beggar's black palm, I have only felt a deliquescence, a shrinking in the clothes that might have its end in the pucker of some last decaying arterial spout, succumbing to the long, dry suction of the grave."

"Delta tells lies," she said, who strode into the circle of listeners as if her canted legs were offering something to be drunk out of the fullness of her hips.

"Delta Tells says that when a gypsy body is interred, each mourner who has physically loved the departed imprints a kiss with such unselfconscious passion that even the lips of the most wizened corpse are made plump with that provocation. Delta says 'It gives the mourner a delightfully lascivious sense of what is meant by the phrase readiness for the grave.'

"But I have noticed the fullness of the lip as the gypsy woman passes. And I have thought that the deceptive sultriness of her pout protruding like nothing so much as the empurpled knuckle of her husband's fist."

"Delta tells lies," she said, who made a show of touching her voice with the tips of her breasts, there was such feeling visibly roused against the nearly permeable material of her blouse by the heft of her breathing.

"Delta Tells says that the gypsy's digestion is a monster of efficiency. He eats everything. Because it is a life unbounded by home and hearth, whatever falls into the pot over an open campfire is naturally suited to the gypsy palate. Taste, for the gypsy appetite is a creature of the world, not of the mouth. It might as well be something hoofed, so swift is the taunt it gives to his hunger. Is this why his mouth never ceases to be open? Nor can it ever be filled.

"Delta Tells says, 'What falls in the way of the gypsy's open mouth, falls into the grip of esophagus. It will bear the imprint of a muscle that flexes in the blood. What is eaten pushes relentlessly downward, compacting a center of gravity within abdominal spaces where the organs would otherwise be whispering to one another in shadowy rhythms of the breath that blows against them all like wind walking on water. The physique thickens with the tremulous contact of membrane wall against membranous tremor of tissue wall, a distention that quickens the gravitational motion of the whole body towards the bowel. The body draws a tightness around its nourishment like the straining of the lips to hold the shape of a kiss. All that passes the lips presses just as suddenly against the sphincter.'

"But I have taken what comes out from between the gypsy's legs to feed an appetite as strong. And, in the caress of my hand, the skin flowed like water. Smoothness rather than fatness was the satisfaction it succored. But smoothness, as the mirror glass shows, puts forth only the image of the body instead of its life.

"Just so, what I have taken in between my own legs, has never come out again on its own two feet."

"Theft of children is the gypsy's vocation, it is said," Brainard Tells heard himself say to his wife. Saying it in the echo chamber of her absence made his hearing more acute. So Brainard did not mind waiting for the face of the white-smocked attendant to recompose itself into a quiet avenue of receptiveness for what else he had to say.

The face of the white-smocked attendant turned from some frustrating ministration over the adjacent bed. The physical concentration of that activity seemed to have closed the already low brow and flattish nose into a heavy fist.

"Who has not heard the stories," Brainard Tells resumed, "of a swarthy skin casting its shadow over the unattended cradle? A moment before it was brimming with sunlight, chirping with the dawn. This is how the gypsy tribe replenishes the life of the road, as if there were no fathers among them.

"And they are so childlike that a father's forgiveness might seem due to them."

The face of the white-smocked attendant still turning to give full attention to these words, wore the twisted expression that went with the cry rising suddenly from behind the avalanche of his shifting shoulders, like something sloughed off into the aisle between parallel bed frames.

Though Brainard Tells was struck down beneath that look, his speech only softened, following its quarry more closely into velvet underbrush.

"Homelessness is the father of lawlessness," Brainard said more quickly, more quietly. "It is the home of childishness, which is the empty cradle of the child himself. See the gypsy face, fat for all the tawdry hunger that hangs about its greying pallor. But look closely. A child's eyes are dancing under the most wrinkled brow. The smile will never uncurl from the wriggle of those purple lips. What looks like the most painfully stooped shoulders are flexed by convulsions of laughter that are the revelation of his skeletal structure, as hard as a finger in your own jocular ribs. Laughter is the string that pulls through the chatter of old bones to make the gypsy spry again."

Again Brainard Tells averted his face from the blow held over him by the white-smocked attendant's wild eyes, though the man's—or woman's, he still had not seen behind the white mask or beneath the hat like a cranial bandage—hands were now lost in the convolutions of some flickering concern with a bright metallic object. Then, seeing—and seeing through—the glass body of the approaching syringe, Brainard Tells tried squeezing his speech tighter as if in that way to evade the needle's fine point, though his arms went up too with the hiss of his words.

"Think. Have you ever seen the gypsy when he is not being jiggled by laughter? Even the palsied hand of the most feeble-looking beggar is a child's pink belly, shaking out its laughter under the ruse of age and decrepitude. There are no limits to the charade because this child grows into a bigger child, however well-swaddled in the clothes of the adult."

Realizing he could no longer see the attendant because the white coat was pressed so closely to his face, Brainard Tells spoke even more breathlessly, as if he were the last mouse whisking his tail under the door, under the bounding shadow of the cat.

"Think. Homelessness is the house of childishness. The fatherless child revenges himself not so much on the absent figure as on the absence of the motive for revenge. In that case the most spiteful revenge is the perpetuation of the life of the child.

"And childishness sired by fatherlessness grows crafty as it grows larger. Just as that part of the body continues to mature—though tragic accident has severed its communication with guiding muscles and nerves—so the child of the road grows ungainly in relation to the world around him. And whether it is an arm or leg, the paralytic limb, however lost to the body to which it is still attached, steals the sight of others.

"So the gypsy steals the child."

The eyes of the white-coated attendant were slit in proportion to the needle's prick where it pierced the word "child." For with a deft motion of the arm that had been folded across his chest, Brainard Tells had removed the flesh. And striking the orderly with the foot that had rested out of sight beneath the white blanket, Brainard heard for himself how the impact to the solidity of the attendant's white gut echoed out of all proportion to the sound of glass sprinkling the floor below them both, though by then the white-smocked attendant had fallen out of sight.

Brainard Tells knew the serum of sleep was already dreaming the floor tiles across which its colorless stain had begun to spread. And though it bristled with the tears of the shattered syringe, he felt emboldened to stand upon that floor as if it were the podium of his dreams.

"So the gypsy steals the child." He struck again with these words, this time lowering himself to the level of his victim, still sprawled between the iron bed frames.

"No mystery is solved in knowing that the theft of children is the most lawless of crimes because it keeps the father at bay. The escaping horse cart leaves the father struck down in its path. The fruit of the cradle will never ripen on the broken bough. I have been struck down. Like you. Like you.

"Do you know 'changeling?'" Brainard put the question into the listener's ear as one lays a coin upon the eye. "Already it sounds like the clatter of the road, does it not? And then the rightful child is supplanted by the rites of perpetual childhood: disobedience, gluttony, sloth, deceit. You shun the gypsy at your door. But when you have met him on the road you will always let him pass by."

Because he was kneeling on the bloody shards of the first syringe, Brainard Tells did not feel the sting of the second. He only heard it in the sudden stillness of his tongue, thickening between his ears until it eclipsed his sight. Before he fell he did not have time enough to look completely over his own shoulder, to see whose hand had put out the light.

But in the last flare of consciousness he was sure that the bed beside his own—and from which he had first distracted the orderly's attention—stared back at him out of the whitest sheets. The bed was empty.

Then the darkness, syphoned around the fading ember of the needle's prick, began to buzz in Brainard's ears like the sense one makes of a stinging sensation if one has grasped it at the hovering bud-end of a tendril which has burst the bubble of its most honeyed scent.

Delta Tells pressed her vertebrae more tightly into the angle of the wall as she opened the wings of the folio-sized volume over her crossed and folded legs. The green, leather-finished end boards of the book set up a tension in the knees where they weighed the heaviest. From the open seam of the binding she plucked a pale satin ribbon that was the memory of where she left off. A musty pollen discharged from the ribbon, taut when she pulled it, the silent note of a melody that played in her head whenever she opened these pages like the lid of a music box coveted from childhood.

Then, the finger that disturbed the translucent vellum sheet—dividing one nacreously colored plate from another—so that it wrinkled like a watery surface, plunged into the velvet socket of *THE HUMAN EYE*. The tight weave of muscles over the bone held her attention like a Chinese finger puzzle, cinched at the knuckle. But pressing still harder against the sheen of the picture and with a single stroke, she unlaced the complex musculature from the frame of the skull just by turning another page.

And then inserting a fingernail along the long thicker edge, on the verso side of the book, she drew back the several layers of cutaneous plastic that had adhered to the vellum divider sheet when she had turned it too heatedly in the anticipation of what she would see. So that she was now staring reflectively into the wet depths of a fully dilated pupil, as if she had turned a faucet instead of a page.

The eye had taken time to see: iris, pupil, cornea, sclera, chorid, retina, optic nerve. The picture was now very clearly the sum of its transparencies, each plastic page pigmented differently with a different physiognomic detail of the organ of sight, each overlaid upon the others, a rainbow palimpsest of impressions which the reader was meant to dissect on more nimble fingertips than hers.

But when she turned the page again, it was quite deliberately *pages* that she moved in a single wave, from right to left, opening up the very middle of the book, now equally divided upon the knees that propped it. The vertex of the intricately stitched binding was sharply aligned with the crotch of her posture. And the weight of the book, conducting a pulse from the knees to the tensile thighs and subtly unseating her from the floor upon which her body otherwise rested, gave her the sensation of hovering over the picture she had exposed.

It was the one picture in the book that divided the contemplative viewer against herself, knowing that as she stripped off the plastic overlays she was emptying that bodily cavity which is breathing room for the most corporeal thoughts.

Though the fetus appeared to be deeply nestled in the womb, its fevered flesh tones germinating in the blush of the uterine wall, it was the first layer to come off, more like a monogram than an implanted organ. It peeled back as softly as the lap of a tongue, though its two dimensions melting into one were the inverse of the relation of the tongue to its taste.

Seen from the other side of the plastic transparency page the image of the fetus, bleeding through, upside down and coiled in sleep, was only a tan stain in the shape of a question mark.

And what remained to be seen on the facing page was not so different from the eye socket: still a nest, however plucked of its egg. The organs surrounding the empty womb were its embrace. And despite their reaching

out for what they no longer held, the lower rib cage like
a filigreed crown, the intestinal fasciae like a cloche over
a heavily powdered face, the kidneys in a skein of arteries
like a sea net, the yellow squash of the spleen illuminating
its collision with the loaf-shaped liver, the sprouting
shards of urethra and fallopian tubes, all peeled away
easily in their turn, until all that remained was the white,
sepulchral ruin of the pelvis like a dry fountain.

This last was a smooth paper page that upon closer
inspection revealed a complex and frenzied pattern of
scratch marks, the incision of a sharp instrument, a fingernail file or a fingernail. Surface and depth could be
held apart if, passing one's fingertips over it, they were
sensitive enough to what was so transparently the desire
to see more. If there was nothing more to be revealed here,
it was nevertheless clearly marked, an excavation site, a
whitening of the page even beyond the bleach of bones
lying exposed to the sun.

Staring into the striations that cross-hatched the
faintly arboreal image of a limbless spinal column rising
abstractly from the smooth bowl of the pelvis, Delta Tells
thought of three more white things:

Below ground, in the coal caverns, old bones had
begun to stir. If, in brittle winter, one took a chef's knife
to the symmetrical hive the wedge-shaped sections would
expose the larval stage, each white mite housed in its
hexagonal armor. As it cools and hardens, the wax that
has been impassioned with the reddish-brownish tint of
human handling reverts to a colorless state.

For each thing there was an admonition:

The bones of extinct monsters, however wildly
they move, are nevertheless, jointed in the head of a man,
she told herself, whose thoughts are far from earth shaking. The larval bees in winter will never mature and will
blacken from first exposure to the biting air. The ball of
colorless bee's wax, white as it may seem, is, in that way,
easily mistaken for the bursting panoply of colors that
harbors the true meaning of the word white.

Brainard Tells awoke with an urgent recollection prying the lid of his skull. More evidence to tell. More that he had forgotten.

"There have been other thefts!" he exploded before he was able to see who was listening. "The gypsy has stood deep in the shadow of other things whose absence was discovered—like the other side of the moon—in a shifting of the light."

In the dark and feathery edges of his vision he spies only the empty beds in wing-like rows on either side of him. Only the ocular window placed high enough in the facing wall that he could not escape his reflection in it. He felt only the shadowy ache of the needle in his upper arm, which cautioned him that *no one* would be his best interlocutor, if he could only be sure that *no one* was here: because he had to speak quite loudly if he would be heard by his wife, distant as he knew her to be from the words that wanted such utterance.

"Who doesn't recall the mystery of a vanished coal wagon? An elephant of pig-iron. Though it must have been strenuously rolled off its track, the wagon itself left no tracks like iron keels in the soft earth. It must have been dragged to an upturned flap of the horizon which no doubt harbors it still.

"A dairyman returning to his cow was unaccountably flushed and feverish to be shrouded in the ghostly bulk of body heat which was all that remained standing in an otherwise empty barn stall, the straw undisturbed, the latches not visibly tampered with.

"The orchard keeper, called early to his work by the unseasonably light soughing of the limbs in the early morning breeze, dropped his jaw to see the branches picked clean. Underfoot, the slow, cud-chewing sound of rotten apples underfoot gave him the scent of the cider he would never taste."

Then as if his voice had been a bell to the band-

aged head of the white-smocked attendant who materialized at his bedside, Brainard Tells was driven faster to the
precipice of his speech. "And the eggs are just as often
gone missing from the chicken house. And the bucket has
disappeared from the well. And the dogs, tethered on
their porches have vanished through the hoops of their
own collars..."

He stopped short before hurling himself off the
edge of consciousness, shoved up to him in the needle's
chromium glare.

"Who has not heard of such incidents, and remembering them in the aura of a vaporous child, who would
not go looking for the child in that direction?"

Then he jumped.

Delta Tells had carried her child unusually high
and frontally, she recalled, as if the fetus were already
reaching for her mind before it was parted from her body.
How could it have known that her mind was already a
nesting place for the body?

The fat textbooks she had clutched against her
stomach through diligent nights of study, heavy as they
were and laden with pictures as full and rounded with
detail as the breath which propped them, had left their
impression. Pages heavy with bodies. Through those books
her mind reached deep inside the bodies of other women
to confer her midwifery officially upon her.

From the day of her certification, fingering the
rough seal embossed on her diploma like the bloody plug
which coagulates as a marker for the neonate's navel,
Delta Tells kept a steady watch at the bearing end of the
birthday bed. In the professional regimen of waiting for
the mountain to fall she taught herself a meticulous
patience. Grains of time passed through the pinch of that
hourglass scrutiny, accumulating the most infinitesimal

knowledge of a woman's body. Everything that a book
had ever prompted her to picture in her mind came
throbbing into her hands. So that in the reaches of time
Delta Tells became known for the gift of turning a woman's
most elusive wants and fears into physical shapes which
the trained hands might comfort, however unyielding the
grip.

Fittingly the conception of her own child came
into Delta Tells' head on her fingertips first, with reverberations of the blow she had struck so coldly against her
husband's cheek. From that moment the thought of conceiving her only child was meant to fit the shadowy form
of her husband's wayward desire. In the penumbra of that
anatomy, she sought the advantage of surprise.

And she succeeded. Though the husband had abandoned his wife's body months before she induced him
into it with words of forgiveness that soured on her
tongue, Brainard Tells realized too late that he had been
meant to find himself there as one who hears a massive
steel door slamming at his back. However involuntary the
emission of his presence inside her might be, he knew that
from this point on it would remember him to himself with
the growing deliberation of one who can no longer be sure
who he is.

And as Delta Tells grew big with the child, she felt
that she had regained the gravitational pull that had
drawn her lover to her breast on the moonlit shores of
their honeymoon idyll, where there had been no mountains to grab at the moon. Now, during the season of her
pregnancy, Brainard Tells returned to his wife at the end
of each day with a tidal regularity, lapping at her needs.
He stood behind her chair at the end of the evening meal.
He put a steady hand against the small of her back when
they walked together on the sloping street. He seemed to
be waiting every morning when she opened her eyes. Even
his lips seemed drawn to her again—however much more
like the snail to the rock than the kisses that suckled her
memory in the sleep from which these kisses awakened
her.

But when the gravitational spell of her pregnancy

was broken by the birth, the orbit of Brainard's attentions became erratic again. Despite the fact that she had slid the newborn into his embrace—her own forearms greased with the labor of extricating the fetal head from the keyhole baffle of pelvis and vagina—Delta Tells felt her husband falling away from her, as if carried off by the weight she herself had conferred.

And the infant's thin flailing cries seemed increasingly disproportionate to the will with which she had conceived his swelling chest and groping arms to be a match for his father's withdrawing body, which was larger and heavier than mother and child combined. When Brainard's silences in her presence embodied themselves in physical absences, thoughts began to clutch at the inner organs of that body which she knew better than he, though he lived upon them, so she said, "like a squatter." For to hold him by this grip she would not even have to extend her reach.

The path of esophagus was charted in her memory in the brown and purple tones of strangulation bruises. By following that path Delta Tells pursued a blue, convolutional uncoiling of the gullet into the violet fundus of the stomach. The fluted swell of the stomach, yellow, aglow, like the rubbed flank of the genie's lamp, lighted the direction of her thinking from there. For the greenish-grayish buoyancy imbued to the stomach by the swirl of intestinal currents foaming beneath it, reminded Delta Tells that just as these imaginary colors lifted the mind off the printed page, hoisting a world of globular bodies, so she had carried her child to term upon the buoyant and nearly globular organs that gave birth to this palette of colors in the official manuals of midwifery. Between the flat world and the round world there was the kinship of their difference. And just as the organs that were the site of ordinary physiological events were shoved into the background of the abdominal theatre in the season of her pregnancy, so in the season of her bereavement she might bring the child into the foreground of her husband's attention again by shifting the props of *his* anatomy.

"Digestion is no less mysterious a process than

birth itself," she tutored herself. So that the invisible weight of the child which she superimposed upon her medical chart vista of esophagus, gullet, stomach and intestine, might be made palpable upon a gullible tongue— if it could only be made to swallow. She knew from the protocol of the throat culture—a midwife must keep a wider view of the body than the Labia Majora allow—that whatever depresses the tongue hard enough brings the stomach directly into the head, even if it is only a pungent eruction of the choke reflex. So she knew a meal could be the lever of her possessiveness. So the husband could be made to carry the child where only the mother possessed the anatomical means to be delivered of it.

And in this way her mind returned to the womb though it was her husband's stomach that consumed her.

She wondered what the stomach could be filled with that might make him cradle it in the arms he no longer extended toward her body. Though these thoughts, which pulled so tightly against the weakly stitched seams of her scalp, made the skull shine more brightly through the thinning features of her face, they were thoughts that solicited a complicated digestion.

To put the child in a man's stomach she would need weight to lay upon the duodenal arch and make it flex. She would require enough irritant in the grain of such a heavy meal to awaken in the intestinal villi the rough texture of the vestigial vitelline. She would need to brew a combustible gas in the ilium, the breath of a rubbery distension that might twist through the gut like the out of step rhythm of the fetal limbs in their dance of development. She would need to weave the capillary strands of the blood into a knot labyrinthine enough to bulk beneath his navel like the first button to come unfastened, before she could expect her husband to become aware of his condition.

But no uterus. No vagina. So she would have to simulate invagination at the other end of the body. She would need a confection poised daringly enough between pepper flake and persimmon to make the fully engorged throat resemble a flexible tube struggling to invert itself at both ends. It would therefore also require something salubrious enough for the tongue so that appetite might override the involuntary contortion of mere musculature, so that the taking it in— from the spur of salivation to the first peristaltic stutter of indigestion—might arouse in his whole body the wriggling sensation that he had in fact *eaten his own.*

Delta Tells felt no embarrassment to ruminate so figuratively that the answer to her husband's question was already *pregnant* inside her, by dint of culinary thoughts alone, and before her husband could ask it: *"What comes closest to being like it, is what it is!"*

Because he had been forced to abandon the search for his clothes, Brainard Tells was that much more cognizant of the prominence of his belly under the loose folds of the infirmary gown, flapping the more freely from the haste of his escape.

His head came through the window first. But he felt the empty expanse beneath him in the flutter of his belly before the rest of him could be coordinated into the motions of a purposeful action that might carry him over it. The gusts of night air forcing the hem of the muslin gown up his skinny legs, where they balanced on the rotten sill, seemed to be reaching for his belly as he prepared to jump. And when he jumped, stubby wings of material briefly and pathetically extended from the disproportionate roundness of his midriff, he fell flat onto his stomach. Though he had taken the height of a man in that leap, he had landed like an animal, a creature that must get up on all fours even to walk on two legs.

Then, running from he knew not what, he felt every sharp edge of stone and thorny stick that paved the way of his retreat imprint itself in the soft white soles of his bare feet. They were picking up weight, slowing him down.

Then he became aware that the preoccupation
with his belly, which he now carried like something he
had stooped to pick up in the heat of a relay race, was
absorbing the pain of each footfall. Or, his belly was
imparting the impact of its own fall to earth on the
thudding balls of his feet.

And he might as well have been the four-footed
beast returned to its wilderness lair when, at last, Brainard
Tells relented in the race against his unknown competi-
tor, finding himself amidst a sudden overgrowth of trees
and bushes and vines which in a few paces would no
doubt have become an impenetrable obstacle. For when
he had dropped to his knees, as if from the weight of what
he was still bearing in his enfolding arms, Brainard Tells
experienced the arousal of the beast surprised in its hole,
though what was springing up before him was an expulsion from his own gut.

Like a miniature self inside him kicking off from
the trampoline membrane of his diaphragm, like the body
bursting from its own shadow, the rancorous spew fleshed
out the shape of his bower in the sour curds of an impasto
that arced as far from his body as he was tall and spread
almost as widely. The foul smell shimmered in the darkness of his bower like a sheet draped over ectoplasmic
stirrings, the ghost of his lost struggle with the peristaltic
strongman who still stood ground within the rattling
shell of Brainard's being.

But his amazement quickly overwhelmed his dis-
gust in the inkling that the wave which had broken on his
tongue was still hanging in the air which it had so satu-
rated, and was even now receding toward him in the
swelling motion of the most unwelcome embrace. Before
he could employ his arms to stay the distance, Brainard
Tells's hands inadvertently perched upon advancing shoulders. Despite its stickiness, he could feel the substance of
the mirage assert itself with a more ominous anthropo-
morphism, though, at the same moment, Brainard Tells
realized that the person, so threateningly in his grip, was
only half his own height and was just as suddenly revealed, in the smeared lustre of the uplifted eyes, to be

only a boy, wiping his face and front as though he were coming through cobwebs.

Brainard Tells could only step back from such a revelation. But the boy kept coming as if in the tow of that mucoid filiation which hung in slack strings between them. And then Brainard himself, forced to step backwards again, lost his balance and fell into the boy's path. The one who had spent himself in the rush to freedom was now underfoot, an impediment and unable to offer anything but the hem of his gown to the horror struck countenance with which the boy demanded to be cleansed of a defilement that had already soaked through his clothes.

Though Brainard's own sense of smell had been blunted, as by a brick, and though the figure standing above him was shrouded in a second skin, rent with holes that evoked nothing so much as the brick of warming cheese, Brainard Tells recognized him. This was a boy who, underneath it all, smelled of wood smoke and whose skin in daylight was dusky enough to want a rag for wiping it clean.

But the boy had already blown past him. The breeze that had coaxed Brainard himself off the window sill made a perfume trail through the darkness. Without thinking, he resolved to follow it as if it were the flowing thread of understanding, looking to pierce the eye of the needle that might give so much obscure pandemonium a point.

Thus unbidden, Brainard Tells was led by his own scent through the befouled night. From above he took the blows of low branches sprung with the faster pace of the boy's invisible passage in front of him. Again, from below, Brainard Tells received the pricks of the rocky terrain which he sensed to be a deliberate evasion of pavement or cobblestone, easements which, by their smoothness, might have given the lead to his feet instead of his nose, taking him in the wrong direction to be sure. From this asceticism he took his sole comfort.

Although he did not know exactly where he was being led (and the leader did not even know himself to be such), Brainard Tells felt that it was right for him to be marching against the currents that flowed toward lighted courtyards and the hubbub of crowded rooms. The nose and the tongue were infinitely preferable to the eyes and the ears, for a man who would be guided to stand at the cook pots and be tested.

For surely now he knew that this was what he was being led to by way of an uncleared path whose only destination could lie on the village outskirts. What, after all, had the boy been doing crouched so low to the ground and so well-camouflaged in the invisible undergrowth, but poaching for the cooks?

At the level of rabbit and squirrel one must be looking for rabbit and squirrel. So Brainard Tells reasoned. And hadn't he already guessed that such was the scale of the deception perpetrated against his palate? Only the brittle delicacy of bones so small could inveigle a thought of plumpness, so well-fitted to the salivations of succulence, that they might cloak the brain in the flesh of the child. Brainard Tells already felt his relief hatching out of the shell of such illusions as he approached what he believed to be the very cauldron of deception itself, where the discriminating tongue might begin, at last, to set things right.

So confident was he of its mission that his tongue began to beat the rhythms of this quick march behind the boy as if the boy himself were the quarry being routed from the bush.

"Bring out your sauces! Unskewer your meats!" Brainard Tells trumpeted ahead of himself, so resonantly and in such adamant tones that the boy leapt that much faster in the stride that could grow no bigger. So, instead of drawing ahead of the raging man, he seemed to draw tight an invisible rope between them. Man and boy burst together into a circle of firelight, as if they had been kicked by the same boot.

At first they were not even recognizable as man and boy. Standing over the kneeling child in his tattered gown, and with his hair teased straight out by the bristly passage through the woods, Brainard Tells presented the appearance of the distraught mother dragging the disobedient child into an arena of punishment.

Only when the amazed circle of log-sitters around the fire were able to decipher the mother's raillery to be an insolent demand for food, and one that was directed at them all, did they take their own charge of the now clearly terrified and mysteriously disfigured child—though one of their own—behind a bulwark of protective arms and a swiftly brandished phalanx of forks and knives.

Brainard Tells saw by the small mounds of broken crockery at their feet, that he had surprised them at their meal, just as he had imagined it. And despite the fact that most of them—men and women alike—now stood taller than was his first impression, he stepped right up to the rattle of their cutlery insisting that he be served.

He saw their teeth first, straining against purple lips in the firelight.

Rage or fear? Feeling suddenly as naked as a tentpole inside the agitated billowing of his loose infirmary gown and realizing that the human circle was closing around him, Brainard Tells sobered into the recognition that *their* rage must be *his* fear.

But it was neither rage nor fear that erupted all around him like circles on a surface of still water, because it was laughter.

Before his relief could slacken the nerves that had cinched so tightly at his tormented waistline, Brainard Tells noticed that some of his hosts still held food in their mouths. He saw that this laughter was a kind of eating which he could enter into inconspicuously. He opened his mouth to join the already boisterous chorus. He was clapped upon the back, heartily, with cheer, though he nevertheless felt a few rogue hands in the cluster probing the folds of his gown for the swaying breasts and featureless groin by which a real woman might have smuggled a false man into their midst.

Then Brainard Tells was being seated. And he complied with alacrity, forcing the curious hands that were trying to inch the hem of his gown above his knees, to pry themselves loose from the splintered crevice closing between Brainard's body and the rough hewn bench where he took his place beside the others. They were men who smelled of the same cooking coal that he had already sniffed off the back of the child whose disappearance he had not yet noticed. Before he could cast an eye backward, a crude table was thrust up to him from the front. It was long enough for six men to dine at, he thought. Six plates and six tin tankards clattered upon the table boards which were as coarse and menacing with splinters as the planks the six ungainly men already occupied and which were rocking like a precarious lifeboat

Brainard's scrutiny however went not to the bristling points of wood, but to the flashing eyes of the women who hugged the food in their arms before they laid it onto the table. As if he could spark some resemblance between what he saw and what he tasted, Brainard tested each bite against the eye-contact evanescing upon the waves of shadow-driven firelight that drew these women into his sights.

He did not look at what he was eating. He let other hands find their way to his compliant mouth, let his own hands wander onto other plates, felt the same ooze between his fingers. In a more fastidious frame of mind, he would have wiped from his lips with a napkin or a shirt cuff.

But there was nothing unfastidious in the eating itself. Brainard let his teeth serve up to his tongue well-masticated portions, distributed equally to the separate quarters of sweet and sour, salt and bitter—and then sluiced away into the gullet to make room for more.

Portions that swelled his memory to the tongue's caress he touched again with his tongue, rolling the substance of faintest familiarity into a ball in order the more easily to revisit the four provinces of taste, the more ready to receive the passionate embrace of recognition if it should fling itself upon him. Even these dry, rounded curds of disappointment, like a thumb pressing against his Adam's apple when he swallowed, heightened the excitement with which he still anticipated the climactic moment of unmasking: when the mysterious flavor that lurked beneath the features of the infant's most fearfully remembered face would stare back at him again. In those puckering eyes and wrinkling lips Brainard Tells had experienced the recurrent cramping of his stomach that was the turbulent wake of his last home-cooked meal.

And all the while he was holding in view the eyes of the serving women who were most certainly the cooks as well. Brainard Tells believed that she who was the mistress of culinary disguises must be watching him back and would unwittingly reveal herself—woman with whom his wife had bartered some knowledge of the body against some knowledge of how to deceive it—in the efflorescent moment of his own illumination.

But it was to be only the moment of his immolation, he conceded, when there were no more shadows to be seen flitting between his face and the firelight, and the fire seemed to exist for no other reason than to show him the other men wiping their fingers on their shirtfronts, as if they were oiling the fat barrels of snub-nosed pistols, indistinguishable from the tight fists that might hold them.

This light, which had been the very filament of Brainard Tells' glow in the orb of night, now seemed to churn inside him, stoking the hold. He had eaten everything, had refused nothing. He had put food in his belly like a man might put a fist in his pocket. Only now would he admit that he had ingested the heat of anger with that of the chili pepper. As a result the blood in which his own stomach was sauced began to boil away until he could smell the scorch marks in his windpipe, began to feel the undulating heat waves rising through his abdomen like reverberations from his diaphragm.

The premonition of what was about to happen roiled within him. It roused the ghost of the absent boy who had led him to the edge of this conflagration and who was now little more than a curl of ash ascending from the chimney of his thoughts. And because he knew that where the ash flies the fire follows, Brainard Tells finally acceded to the molten eruption from his belly for the second time in one day. This time he wished only to follow a law of Nature, and in becoming part of a natural event, to revel in the loss of self-control.

But even on his knees, at the edge of the fire, and with the force of convulsions compelling a preternatural communication between his hips and his shoulders, pushing him onto all fours again, making him all the more simple, Brainard Tells realized that he was dousing the very flames in which his meal had flickered with such significant portent. Worse yet, the tastes which he had sifted so meticulously upon ingestion evoked, upon re-gurgitation, exactly the semblance of recognition he had hunted at the bounteous table, but which he knew would be blotted from his memory by this cruel mimicry of its elusive knowledge, from which only the darkness itself issued any more.

Those who heard the story with their own ears could not dispel the blood from their faces, as if they were rouged with the knowledge of another woman's shame.

"Delta tells lies," she said, who let the dryness of her lips be heard in her speech like a silent request.

"Delta Tells says that the gypsy diet is strictly aphrodisiac. Our own bodies would be too squeamish for the taste that tickles, she says. But the gypsy body is made to vibrate at a different pitch.

"For example: the heart of a chicken, sweated in mustard, will make a woman's breasts rise without being touched. 'Gripped by their own nipples,' she says. 'And then they *will* be touched, because they cannot be resisted.

"'Or', she goes on, 'the foot of a pig, soused in a horseradish vinegar is known to bring about a tightening of the foreskin, to arouse a burning sensation, an imagin-able liquefying of the skin. Whatever moves inside the male member then, like the flicker inside the flame, lights up the face as well.'

"But the acrid fumes which have wafted to my own nose from the open grills of the gypsy encampment tell me that livers and kidneys, gizzards and lungs, are the only organs to which the gypsy cooks apply an ardent flame. These organs are the body's bad breath. And unlike the notorious smells that are thrown off like sparks from the act of lovemaking, the mouth from which they are expelled was never meant to be opened."

"Delta tells lies," she said, who hugged herself when she spoke as if the words wriggling to be free were a wave of heat escaping from her body.

"Delta Tells says that the stamina of the gypsy lover is matched only by the appetite of the woman he serves: 'And the gypsy woman never places a napkin on her lap to prepare for the meal. She eats without underwear!' By the jaunty look in her eye, I know that she has meant for her pouting mouth to mimic the pucker of elastic she has so purposely fingered at my waist, however casually she has dressed that gesture in a sisterly pat.

"Delta Tells says the women of the campfire rise with the flame of their ardor above the prostrated man. It is a position which she assures me is known to us only in the act of micturating behind a bush. If I desire to question the truth of this, she warns me to heed the calves like well-oiled pistons and the rippling thighs of the women who are unashamed to hoist their skirts above the music of the dance.

"But I have seen the gypsy women trudging under their loads of wet firewood. It is their feet we see, never their legs. And their feet, shaggy with mud and grass might as well be hooves planted against the backward motion of a wooden cart, dragging them back to the earth."

"Delta tells lies," she said, who probed the depth of her shadow with one foot, as if to tease a body of water that holds no threat of drowning.

"Delta Tells says, 'The gypsy's orgasm, true to the spoonerism that mocks it in its own lair, is an *organism* apart from her other natural faculties.

"'When it springs from the loins of the true gypsy,

it makes its own rustling in the air, bristles its own fur, sounds its own noises. Once it has leapt it will never return to the place where its nostrils first flared. No nest. No searching its own smell. Only animus, animate.' Delta Tells says that the moment of sexual climax for the woman of the road is the moment when the fox is out.

"But I have walked past the open horse cart parked deliberately, yet indiscreetly behind a thin screen of trees. And however moist with passion, the tell-tale cries that quickened the rhythm of that motionless buckboard were indistinguishable from the even more familiar hoarseness, laden with sour apples and rotten tubers which I hear the gypsy market-crier struggling to throw off above the voices of the other vendors, who, unlike herself are growers not foragers."

The oldest and deepest shaft of the mine was unnumbered, but bore two names that glimmered up from the still well-polished depths of inlaid brass plaques: *LEOPARDI'S LUCK!* and *CATASTROPHE OF 1931.* Though the clatter of picks and pails which catches the rhythm of the miner's vocation had been officially silenced at the gate, the octagonal opening to the shaft—heavy timbers set into a bare rock face—buzzed continuously with the voices of men and women gathered all day to wait their turns.

They were admitted—two at a time—to descend, to peer through isinglass darkness, to bear witness to the progress of the excavation from behind sagging ropes that smile insidiously upon the jagged abyss of time separating the disoriented couples, from the efficient white-smocked archeological workers beyond.

But when Delta Tells was sighted cresting the hill where the mine entrances clustered above pedestrian streets, those in the throng who had impatiently waited their turns, casually dispersed. They were demonstrably giving way, demurring the sight of what they had anticipated only too well because they had seen it before, that they might see more covetously, the expression on this woman's face after she viewed the scene of her husband's disaster. The lantern-helmeted officials in white laboratory coats still called it "the lucky find."

The lapidary sounds of chiseling and sweeping that arose like a fine dust from the far side of the ropes were precise miniaturizations of the miner's heavy labor, though the objects the archeological workers exposed to view dwarfed even the labyrinthine distances of tunnel that made of the mine an unreachable destination.

As Delta Tells approached, she was innocent of her husband's stealthy gaze, his eyes in the back of her head. From behind the jutting edges of buildings, from behind a slow-moving automobile passing a horse cart in the opposite direction, from behind militant hedge rows and now from behind the wrought-iron gatepost that dropped heavy shadows across the path he followed, Brainard Tells did not lose sight of his wife's purposeful figure until the ranks of the curious, closed smartly behind her when she entered the mine and the sounds of the shaft elevator's descent threatened to draw the earth out from beneath his feet. Yet it didn't shake his gaze.

"Obedient to the rule of two, the only other passenger plummeting to the depths seizes Delta's hand at the first lurch of the elevator carriage, as it disappears inside the ring of silent watchers. Relaxed as she is in her abandonment of the daylight, Delta lets her hand be taken as well. Then, like something predatory sensing vulnerability in its prey, the collapsing floor of the elevator takes her feet and her stomach as well.

"When the two women bump hard against each other under a spark of light that might have been struck between two stones—it throbs in both their heads—they understand they have arrived at the bottom of the shaft. Here the light is constant, but reflected so unevenly from the rough iron-hewn walls of the tunnel that it seems to shine upon them through

the ragged teeth of a cracked eggshell.

"The archeological workers, on whom the light is focussed, ignore the inaudible approach of the two women. The workers seem to be figurines sealed in the spherical bliss of a child's glass ball, though the dust that hangs over their labors looks as much like the precipitate of a hammer blow against the hard glare of the overhanging bulb as like a silent snowfall.

"Because the two women are still holding hands, all their other movements go in tandem, sweeping them twice as quickly into the embrace of the red velvet ropes, hanging slack between tarnished brass stanchions, and placed at a vantage point for the choicest view, as if to summon the luminous spectacle they graced long ago in the ruined motion picture palace from which they were plundered.

"The twinning effect of the women's synchronous gait seems to coalesce into a more primitive physical bond when they at last stand still behind the ropes as if grown together in one another's intertwining arms. The arms are webbed with shadow and therefore cast a more monstrous shadow upon the sight they survey, if anyone would look up to see what is flapping such black wings to roost above their heads.

"But the archeological workers' eyes are scattered over the floor of the tunnel like the bits of bone and rock they sift on sensitive fingertips. Standing on their knees, they seem deliberately dwarfed to the scale of their specimens. Yet with a simple snap of the head, telescoping to a greater focal length, the shrewd eye for detail would see at once how the minutely particulated rock on which the three workers numb their kneecaps, reticulates into a vast and suddenly animate mosaic: haunches broad as an elephant, stubby lizard paws extended to the reach of a tree branch, jaws the length of a horse's head, all heaving against the shuddering eyeball of incredulity, like the surprising self one meets upon walking through plate glass.

"'It is the creature about which all have read as children, whose commonly unpronounceable name is crowned with the mnemonic Greek for king and whose flesh—in all the illustrated books that children pass between them—is painted an atavistic brown, the better to clash with the indolent green *of the plant eaters. The saurus suffix flicks these childhood memories, teasing the fears that snakes and dragons tickle with the same forked tongue.'*

"This informative reverie is proffered over the ropes to the spectators' nibbling lips. It passes in hushed words between two women's faces when they inexplicably turn away from what can be seen under a bright light. Or else the long lisping sound that suckles such a thought really is the kiss which the sight of their closer embrace (if anyone would see it) makes the more irresistible thought. That thought composes this picture: two grief-struck women stand face to face, their plaintiff arms flung over each other's shoulders like the wings of an abortive ascent. The silhouette of their commiseration is cut by the razor-sharp light incising the revelation of fossil remains behind them.

"But what kind of grief is this?

"If Delta Tells has pressed the absent child into a stranger's embrace, has finally unburdened herself of the secret of the child's secreting, if her own child's heart has been flicked by the lizard's tail, prompting her to confession, and so to the actions of the good mother, then why are the other woman's hands fluttering up and down this good mother's back as if to seize a snake from her spine? Why does the good mother permit the other woman's brown leg to twine slowly around her calf and ankle and by that advantage of gravity to lever her backwards into a deeper embrace? Why in this position does the good mother permit the slow movements of her own face against the other predatory face to fall into a rhythm with the movements of her lower body, caught as it is at the fork of her legs by the brown woman's strenuously raised knee?"

These were the questions that throbbed behind Brainard Tells' eyes as he inched his head out from shadowy cowl of his hiding place to see his wife emerge from the more labile shadows of the mine's interior. The shawl that had all but covered her face when she entered was now flapping at her waist. No one followed her. Nor did she turn her head to see.

Her movements, so miniaturized and so quickened by the distance her husband stood apart from her, made

Brainard Tells think that this volatile figure bustling beyond the brightly highlighted hexagonal frame of the shaft entrance fairly buzzed to be free of the honey-combed hillside, which men had flocked to like ants.

She must have been there, lingering in his path like his own footprints. Brainard Tells guessed that as he had followed her, so she would have been capable of following him. He had been followed from the moment he remembered a faint syncopation of his footfall, like something stuck to the sole of his shoe, dragging his gait. But his memory of this came later.

And it was in the memory that he began to think of himself as *her* shadow, though the events remembered, freighted *his* body with the wearying inertia of a man who gathers physical weight with every step he takes.

Before memory he had felt the lightness of his own body to be the spring of all his actions. His spirit was the release from the body's physical compression. This gave the easy, natural motion to his infidelities, which was the flatly stated explanation he had tendered to his wife's suspicious nature.

He had felt the account to be true before he remembered it to be so, though he now remembered it differently.

He had left the bedroom door ajar behind him, in that way putting on the disguise of his return even before he had departed. But that gap was a hole for a suspicious wife to slip through the nets of her husband's most deceitful calculation, even as his whole person occupied the space in which he contemplated it.

Later he wondered that because he had not lingered with it, she herself must have entered this thought like a door.

By then, he had moved out into the night, nimble

steps ahead of her that must have been numbered in her mind if she were to keep a safe distance between them. He himself was mindful only of the space and not the time in which he traversed it. Space was the medium of his delight from the moment he immersed himself. The exposure of his lightly covered shoulders and bare head to the evening dampness was urgently contiguous with moist palms whose touch he anticipated would mottle his warm chest and cool forehead as if he were a pane of glass dividing two temperature zones. He enjoyed the transparency of his presence in the perfectly opaque darkness, walking briskly, flawlessly down a notoriously crooked street, joyously alone, though now he remembered a faint syncopation of his footfall, like something stuck to his shoe, dragging his gait.

That sound too must have been swept forward in the stream of his stride, like something he might find rolled to the bottom of the hill when he reached the end of his descent.

But halfway to the bottom of the dank and vertiginously twisting cement stairwell that was the place of assignation—a gurgling drain rising to meet him—he floated into the aura of a woman whose breathing was as regular as the waves.

He had found his way so quickly from the top stair, by letting his body swing freely between the wrought-iron hand-rails on either side, and as smoothly as if an iron bar ran laterally through his shoulders, stiff as the muscles in each straight arm that braced him against a headlong fall. Swiveling on that axis he felt the monkey fur dampen in his armpits.

As on all other such occasions, Brainard Tells had found the woman where he sought her, by following her instructions. But the exact destination always remained a mystery to him until he took the last prescribed turn on the intricate track she would have laid out before him in advance. Even then she would always manage to be there in place of the place to which her instructions would have led, had she not stood in their way herself. She was always one step ahead of him, so he would never know where he might have ended up. But this time, a beat before their hearts would have touched, he guessed he had arrived at the basement entrance of a building that in the daylight was illuminated on one wall, with the glaring white letters P H Y S I C A L   P L A N T. The heavy breathing of generators behind a closed door made him think "the lungs of the mine" which he knew communicated with the many tunnels into which the miners descended, through other tunnels.

What he did not know and could not have expected was that the metal-reinforced door with its square window that waited, so he thought, to be opened just beyond the drain at the bottom of the well, had nothing whatsoever to do with his entering the woman who hovered so provocatively in the space between.

For his last step down to her was *not* the last step in the stairwell, and the first contact he made was not with the breasts that would have breathed softly against his sternum but with a short jab of her pelvic bone.

His hands meeting her naked feet on the hand rails confirmed for him the ingenious posture that was not available to sight but which he comprehended at once in the uncanny fit it made with his groin, like the snout of a friendly dog. She did indeed prop herself up on the rails with her hands. But her hands gripped the handrails *behind* her feet, so that her straight arms made the frame of a phantom chair back against which she could lean her whole body, thrusting her head back into the deeper darkness beneath her shoulders and thrusting her sex forward between her knees like the fox darting from the bushes.

Her naked body was configured in such a way that had he been naked himself, and aroused by this image of unstinting physicality, he would have stepped inside her body more easily than stepping through the door to which she so yieldingly blocked his access.

Though now he remembered a faint syncopation of his footfall, like something stuck to his shoe, dragging his gait. But then he had not thought to stop short in his tracks in order to sift out the lurking presence behind him from the absorptive silence that gaped palpably in front of him.

He remembered only pushing forward, wondrous at the permeability of his clothing, the propitious opening and closing of seams, the dilating of pores, the sensation of being both barbed and caught on the barbed end of himself like a thread whose tautness threatens to tear the very stillness it demands of the whole body, stiffening not to make a bigger tear.

In the next instant, Brainard Tells heard the glottal flap stopper a cry that sucked at the woman's windpipe, just as her bare feet levitated from the hand rails, so that now she was supported only by the pale column of blood that spewed from between his legs and just as mysteriously became a tourniquet inside her.

In the unstoppered sound of a clicking heel that now played through the remembered interval of that woman's audibly held breath, Brainard Tells' consciousness of another person who must have stood on the steps behind him then resonated with the timbre of his wife's name. He was himself a gong to the thought striking him now, that then he had stood between two women, one imploring him to remember, the other imploring him to forget where he was.

Then he had taken another step down, toward the thrum of the generators pumping robust chestfuls of blue air into the branching shaftways of the mine.

Now, hearing it above the sound of the generators, Brainard Tells realized that *then* the breathing in his ears had been loud enough for two women who would have been closer to each other than either could have known because he stood between them.

Then he had been conscious only of standing between one of them, he had entered her so deeply, driven her apart.

But now he remembered the other one. He felt the presence of the other one, pressing moist palms upon his back.

Or how else could he have felt the perspiration from his sodden shirt back soaking back into his skin?

And how else could he have lost the balance proffered to him by the brusquely elevated, feathery knees, beating the air around his flanks, flying against the arc of the woman's body falling away from the contrary curve of his chest? How else could the broken-winged bird that was their union then have flown so crookedly down the dozen remaining steps of the stairwell and pitched, with the velocity and direction that drove the woman's head straight through the square window of the locked door? It bared its teeth at the moment of impact and buried them in the cleft beneath her jaw.

Holding the woman's violently straightened legs in his hands like the poles of an upended wheelbarrow he felt the livid mouth that yawned in the whiteness of her throat snap shut on the burrowing end of himself still moving inside her, stretching its snout toward a far wall where the tiniest giggle of her girlish self still waited, in the euphoric darkness, to be touched.

He smelled blood. He heard the glass teeth fall from the steel jaw. He was shattered himself. But he could not extricate the smallest part of himself from the iron maw of catastrophe no matter how he moved his feet on the resonant concrete steps, though he now remembered a faint syncopation of his footfall like something stuck to the sole of his shoe, dragging his gait. Now he was sure that those phantom footsteps were actually escaping behind him, running as he was in the opposite direction, though he could not move.

Fading against the pace of his own struggle with the locked door—which would have been the key to releasing himself from the skew-limbed corpse, which he now inadvertently crushed at the bottom of the stairwell—the sound of his wife's heels, clicking above his head and against a damp pavement, echoed back in his memory to trod on the softer features of his face, as wet with his tears as the thunderstruck ground.

The wife turned against her husband in bed, front to back, the better to whisper into the dark drain of his ear.

She had not expected to awaken beside him. More frequently it was only the brittle impression of his body that remained in the soft shale of the mattress, a trail of prehistoric footprints in a dry lake, brought to the surface of her consciousness when she spread her fingers out over the buoyant darkness in a dream of swimming from which she never awoke with a splash. But this time her hand did come back wet.

Fever? For no other reason could she imagine that her husband would have trembled at her touch. For no other reason could she imagine that he would have left this chilly remnant of himself chattering beside her while the night was warm and deep beyond the uncharacteristically secured latch on the bedroom door.

This was the spark of her anger: that he would give up his body like a chore to be done by her, a fever to be cured, a pot to be cleaned. He had deposited the sick body—it had not laid naked beside her since the cries of childbirth had broken upon their sleep like the rafters of a new day—without speaking to her, without even gesticulating a request. As cold and waxen as his back was to her touch, so she resolved to light this candle at both ends.

The word she applied to his ear, in a heated whisper—"Sire!"—was accompanied by a deft thrust of one hand between his legs. She entered him from behind, where the oval parting of his thighs made a soft sigh, the only murmur of life from his side of the bed. She let her touch linger long enough for his breath to catch on it. Then she seized the front of him, only to pull him back through the opening that was still holding the shape of her delicate wrist. She might have been pulling his tongue out between clattering rows of teeth, to hear the sound of his pain so throttled and inarticulate.

He reached for himself with both hands only to

discover the bare pubic bush burning between his legs. He felt the pain tearing up in his eyes like grains of salt rubbed into the blurry slits. The slack length of his penis was stretched across his perinaeum, a goose neck helpless on the block, the head, still tight in the wife's irate fist and lashed in the chrism of his buttocks.

The sweat of his fever was shed convulsively by the sweat of his suffering, and something reptilian emerged in the coarsening grain of the skin where it was drawn and worried against the pelvic saddle.

Suddenly he knew he was in the fetal position. Even through the fog of his fever and in the blistering of his pain he sensed a rightness in knowing that if one pulled hard enough upon the penis it produced the posture of the fetus like an elastic strap recoiling upon itself.

But the wife's satisfaction came from knowing that he was in a posture of child bearing. His chin cleaved to his breastbone. His shoulders beckoned helplessly toward the embrace of his buttocks. His thighs, close enough to his head for a whisper to pass audibly between them, quivered like the fleshiest lips, feverish to speak.

But between his thighs, where all the effort and pain were focused with the heat of the blind magnifying glass that was his brain, there was neither a peering protuberance or a liquid socket. Pared of his sex, he had not been laid open. He was sealed up and bursting to expel his own searing center of gravity.

Instead the husband himself was extruded from the consciousness in which his pain was clenched. And when the husband's cries at last were silenced—in the plush, black, swaddling of the comatose—the wife commenced to baby him.

The basins of his fever, where his consciousness collected, were oases, where his every need was ministered to. Delta Tells shook the thermometer down from its raging heights. She flooded the dry pathways of his body with liquids, soaked up the run-off from his forehead and armpits, kept the bedclothes brimming at his chin.

After the fever broke Brainard Tells was allowed to float in his bed. No destination imposed on the languid currents that carried him. No anchorage. Except for meals.

At first the meals were simple enough to be carried to his bedside in one hand. A tribute to the delicacy of his organs: dry toasts, the pulp of an orange. The food she brought was like the tidbits that one holds out of an open doorway to inveigle the cat's return.

When he had recovered the strength to reach out for it himself, she strengthened the fare: eggs, whole fruits, cheese, the skinless breast of a chicken.

When he was ready to sit up she propped the softer tissue kneaded by his appetite with fiber and bone: celery stalk, rutabaga, a shoulder of pork, a butt-end of beef.

When he thought he was strong enough to walk unaided, she told him that one meal remained which would certify his clean bill of health. He should not refuse it. She cautioned that the mind always raised itself before the body was able because it was above eating. She reminded him that a fever refuses nourishment in its ascent. She had rescued him from that cloud before it carried him too far aloft of the needs that only a well-stoked stove top could satisfy. She told him that a man needs to feel the tether of his duodenal knot if he is to let his thoughts balloon about his head without fear of where they might take him.

She would return to the stove. For his part, she ordered him to lie still in his bed until he felt the tingling dilation of his nostrils and—inhaling the rich aroma from the kitchen—he drew as much bulk against the ciliate membranes as if it were his tongue that itched to be discharged from his nose when he breathed. Then he should permit himself to be led by the nose to this final test of digestion.

Then she promised that the cook would be the midwife of his gustatory pleasure. She promised that despite the fact he had not walked in two weeks, he would not remember how he had come to his place at the table. The flavors on his palate would seem to have been a magical transport. The palette of her flavors would be sufficient reason for swallowing any explanation. He would be so entered into the scene of his banquet, when it entered him, that he would not ever want to leave.

"It is a feast for a king," she told her husband when she set the heavy iron pot before his place. And because he ate regally, with his back straight, his head high, though he was dipping into the very bottom of the pot, he must have believed that it was true.

When he was finished she saw that he had no need of the napkin. He had licked himself clean. His lips glistened with satisfaction. She waited for the smile to gnaw its way through the plumped mouth.

Then she spoke.

"**Y**ou have eaten your own." These words were knotted in Brainard Tells' gut when he was awakened by the memory of the previous night. The thought was a rind of gristle caught in the meshes of his digestion. He seemed to find the spot with his hand pressing for the shape of resistance along a yielding muscle wall where the abdominal cavity verges upon the groin. A pulse of warmth. A slippery nodule. If he could keep his grip on it he felt he might at least still the tongue of the accusation.

"You have eaten your own." If he had reached into his wife's mouth when she had first uttered those words and seized the clapper of her report, he would not have needed the grip he was now losing to some subcutaneous viscosity of the skin which had so evasively outlined his innermost fear.

The pain that smoothed to impalpability between his pincer fingertips remained beneath the surface of his belly, unreachable. Where his fingers had failed however, the groping of his consciousness for something that had slipped the glassy surface of familiarity yielded the awareness that he was still a fraternizer at the gypsy encampment.

Licking his lips, he rekindled the spark of the meal

that had been fanned from a red pepperflake the night before. As if by the light of its heat, he could see himself silhouetted at the long table where he had ingested the very bellyache that had just dredged him from his deep sleep. If he could not seize the pain between his spidery fingers, at least he had the shape of it in the remembrance of this image, though he was seeing it now for the first time. This was his own. But still he did not know what he had eaten.

And then opening his eyes for the first time he saw that nothing else was his own. He had even lost the white shift in which he had fled the infirmary bedclothes, ghostly clasp, of his last dream-molested sleep.

But now the bed in which he was so confusedly reposed became a cradle of recognition. Because he was not alone in it. He was lying between two women whom he could not have mistaken as the cooks of the previous night's banquet. They had cuddled the meal to his table in the same arms that were now strung together like a loosely tied bow around his shoulders and neck, the only semblance of a garment that remained to any of them.

Turning back and forth from one sleeping face to another, his vision overlapped in the realization that the women were twins, one the perfect impression of the other's sharp features, as if the turning of his face between theirs was the medium of malleability in which the intaglio meets the image of its mirroring relief.

Neither one her own, he thought. They were obliged to look between them for their nature. And there Brainard Tells lay with his bellyache still stirring, where the meal served out of the companionable hands of these dream-sloughed women, still taunted the nimbleness of his fingertips.

When he looked back at them, one after another, he remembered how the night before they had impetuously welcomed the proposal that he taste their tongues alternately to see if *they* could tell the difference in the same way. He himself sought a finer distinction and felt guiltless in his guile. He had clucked silently to himself that two women with the identical tongue proffer, to the

man who would tell the difference between them, only
the otherwise unattainable uniqueness of his own being.
If he could not tell what it tasted like to have eaten his
own, he would at least—and indubitably—own the instrument of his taste.

But this too was denied him.

Invited now to enter the mouth of the one who
awoken first, he allowed his face to brush close. He
opened his own mouth and closed his eyes. His own
mouth was a humid cave resonant with low-pitched animal cries. Inside the cave his tongue hung back, tasting
blood before he knew he had been bitten.

The click of her teeth inside his own jaws had
snipped the frail thread by which his body dangled from
his brain, dispossessed him of whatever thought would
have moved him toward the object of his own desire.

He was still so close to the nuzzling face that he
saw things out of her eyes. Or he would not have caught
sight of the other sister passing behind him, bearing into
the blind spot that was his own head the same face which
his immersion in the mirroring eyes obliterated from his
vision. When this face reappeared, it was in the binocular
embrace she restored to him, by rotating to her sister's
other side. But in the blur of shifting focal planes the one
who had bitten his tongue withdrew and the one who had
disappeared behind his head came forward, reached out
to take his head in her hands, begging, as he knew, the
same compliance from his salt-stricken mouth.

Now she sat back down upon the bed. Applying
him to a nipple so erect it might have been driven into her
like a spike into the sugary heart of a maple trunk, she
teased the shape of the spigot that watered at his lips.
Then Brainard Tells understood how the sweetness of the
sensation flowed not in but out of him, an involuntary
motility budding at the tip of his tongue.

She held him by the ears. When she had waited no
longer than it would take for a jug to fill under the spigot,
she loosened her grip. Her hands moved in the shapeless
motion of a rag brought to soak up a spill. Her hands were
moving over his eyes. They were pushing against his face

but without any intent of turning him away. Then she leaned back onto a gentle wavelet of bedding, forcing him to ebb upon the opposite current, leading him whither.

When his face had drained into the hollow of her pelvis, she began to exert further pressure on the back of his head, as if she were tamping handfuls of earth into a narrow furrow. The pressure, gathering in her fingertips, prompted his tongue to recognize an analogous protuberance out of the tight crevice which was the bottom of the furrow.

Suddenly the slipperiness of the contact that had made him think he had penetrated a blind socket with his tongue welled up inside his mouth with the tears of a bitter salivation. He would not swallow, but the bitterness rose on the back of his tongue as if tethered to the bucket in a bottomless well of bitterness.

And as if she were only about the business of drawing fluids into available containers she began to push once more against his burning forehead, canting her hips more vertiginously, disengaging the spigot from the spout.

But this time he did not wish to follow her lead or to yield to the weight of her hands that were now the most persistent thoughts pressing on the top of his head. Because now she was pushing his face deeper between her legs toward the place where a sour breath lisping about a pair of sniggering lips threatened the most malevolent kiss.

It was to avoid the kiss that he parted his own lips to speak and inadvertently endured the far more unsavory intimacy of the *tongue* with the rectum.

His head broke free of her grip, as if he would use it to strike her back. He wielded himself as a blunt instrument intending to gather weight in the violent upswing that was effected by rising to his feet. But he did not bludgeon her with the outrage that whistled through his nose like an axe head swooping through the dark.

Instead he let his head come to rest in his hands, full of the knowledge that he, who had sought to extend himself by the salubrious reach of his tongue had been sewn mercilessly into the skin of that rough-skinned organ. Salt, Sweet, Bitter, Sour. These were the four walls which held him after the maze of excitations through which the woman had led him.

Her laughter was guttural. Free of the tongue. When she propped herself on bare white arms the teeth seemed to drip from her upper jaw. She had let the water run in her head. Her hilarity flowed out to him, a tide that threatened to bear him away like the nose of land sticking too far out into a wild current.

And, having been so definitively reduced to his body, Brainard Tells lost the feel of it. It was the numbness that envelopes the site of a compulsive touching and he would have gladly let himself sink beneath that surface without a trace. But there were physical forces yet to be reckoned with.

Again from behind him, the second sister materialized into his line of sight. Orbiting him, until she eclipsed his view of her sister on the other side, this second sister, coming the second time around, proffered more than herself in the place of the first.

Still naked, she cradled an armful of clothing. With one gesture of her long arms she divided it into two offerings, a yellow leather-fringed shirt in one hand, a pair of striped flannel trousers in the other. Though he might have accepted it as propitiation of his still burning indignation, Brainard Tells knew at once from the sheen of wear, winking at the flapping elbows and flickering knees, that this was merely a perpetuation of the insult. For she proposed nothing less than to dress him in the clothes of a dead brother.

Even as Brainard Tells hastened—however ambivalently—to fill the orifices of the clothing with the shivering parts of his body, he breathed with foreboding the comparatively warm breath of the departed. The smell of mothballs beat tiny wings above the commotion of his dressing. But underneath it was the broad, reclining odor of flaking skin, dried body fluids and an ammoniac charge to the atmosphere that quickened the action of everyone involved.

The laughing woman appeared to have been pro-
pelled from the bed to join the effort with her sister: four
hands straightening snaggly seams over the points of his
narrow shoulders, hoisting a raggedly knotted waistband
above his angular hips, rolling deep cuffs free of his
ankles. They drew crimson felt slippers over his bare white
feet, lassoed his neck with a green paisley bandanna, and
to finish, tossed the solid weight of a gold timepiece into
his front pocket so that it chimed painfully against his
testicles.

Only after he was completely dressed and the
sisters stood apart from him as if releasing him into the
embrace of a beckoning mirror, did he realize that they
were in fact revealing him to a hidden presence in the
room.

Because he followed their eyes away from the
ridiculous figure he cut between them, he could see that
behind the stack of broken-staved barrels that teetered
toward him as he looked more closely, or behind the
vaguely oriental dressing screen shot with holes that
winked at his disbelief, or from behind the beaded curtain
that breathed into the back of the room, someone had
been waiting to come out.

Nor did the sisters make a move to cover their own
nakedness—it stood out against enclosing shadows like
freshly poured milk—when, from a sudden shifting of the
same shadows a man who could only have played the role
of the father, shambled forward to close the family circle.
He possessed the indeterminate height of a growing boy.
His pants swept the floor as he walked. The loose sleeve-
ends of his garishly stained morning coat flapped behind
his back and over the hands that were invisibly clasped
inside them. The hands hitched under the last vertebrae,
tilted him forward in his gait so that he had the look of a
man carrying his own head on a spike that weighed
painfully across his sagging shoulders.

Then the small, round face festooned with white
beard and moustache floating up into Brainard's fasci-
nated gaze revealed the proverbial man within the child,
and with a candor that was all the more shocking because

the smile that was creased in the papery skin and the short arms that drew Brainard's head down into a close embrace belonged unmistakably to the child's exuberance.

But the voice that uttered the word "Sonny" when Brainard stooped close enough to hear the beating of his heart, was a whiff of the grave: carious teeth, rancid saliva, worm-crannied bones.

Running away as impetuously as he had burst into their midst, Brainard Tells knew, in the still raw and resonant knuckles of his fist, that the mouth which seemed to have yawned so cavernously in the foul breath of the old man's speech had been broken open like the ceremonial clay pot in which a pharaoh's intestine has fermented for five thousand years.

The fist was Brainard's own.

Those who heard the story with their own ears expelled the breath that was snagged on it with increasingly slow and regular contractions of the diaphragm.

"Delta tells lies," she said, who fondled her knees, feeling for where to loosen the entanglement of her crossleggedness, as if she might find the full stride of herself in a posture otherwise pulled tight and hobbled with the tension of what she had to say.

"Delta Tells says that a woman must cook for her husband if she wishes to keep him at home. She says that the pungency of the kitchen should lock in the nostrils like a ring of steel. She says she has learned much from the gypsy cooks. She has learned that even the grip of steel can be broken if the man himself is not hungry.

"'Perfect the art of hunger,' she says, 'and you will enjoy the perfect marriage.'

"But I have fed my husband well, and if *mine* has not, *his* belly has blossomed with our love. Because the life that stirs within it once wriggled on the tines of a fork

I am confident of the grip that holds us together."

"Delta tells lies," she said, who wormed a finger through an empty buttonhole of her blouse as she felt for the words she wanted with the lump in her throat.

"Delta Tells says that the waywardness of the unfaithful husband is veritably an organ of his body. And it is an organ indifferent to the evolution of his species. It is vestigial of tropisms that guided the flesh before the brain tissue fluffed up inside his head like the white wig with which a foppish gentleman used to crown his vanity.

"She says that if a doctor were to examine this organ for its health, he would find it by putting one finger down the throat while exerting enough pressure between two fingers gripping the base of the scrotal sac, to make the patient swallow.

"But my Olaf is faithful beyond question. And there is no mystery about his body that I have not solved with the smoothness of my touch. Besides, all the organs of his body are quite up to date, a fact which the tirelessness of his lovemaking declares with indefatigable candor."

"Delta tells lies," she said who compulsively caught at a single blond curl dangling over her eye, caught it and released it as if she might be plucking the thoughts from her words as she spoke them.

"Delta Tells says that every husband has an appetite that his wife cannot fill. This is because they are both made in such a way that the man fills the woman up unequivocally. What she places in his stomach does not balance the equation. It only adds to the weight of the world, of which he is thereby made a bigger part. She says, 'This is the problem between men and women: the man carries himself in his body. And in that way he weighs with the world. The woman is part of the world by omission. Her hunger, unlike his, leads out of the world, never in!'

"But I have always lived in the world. Standing under the predictable sun, I cast a reliable shadow. If I step across my shadow I do not fall into an abyss. Instead it disappears in one stride between my scissoring legs, the

same place where the man, so prepossessing in his bodily
assertions, vanishes from the light of day, though he
thinks he sees where he is going."

As he had done so many deceiving times before,
Brainard Tells leaned silently against the bedroom door,
exerting only the pressure that would be required for
deafening the ears with a pinch of cotton wadding. In all
the remembered times past, when his entry into the room
had coincided with daylight breaking through the glass
panes scintillating on the opposite flank of the marriage
bed, he had proved himself adept at jumbling the motion
of his wife's waking with the motion of his own fleet form
sliding under the covers. Even as she was throwing them
off. He told himself that the blur of dawn's light refracted
through the glare of her half-open eyes made such a ruse
possible.

But this time he was the one awakened—from the
trance of running which had swept him home from the
gypsy encampment in a single wave of perspiration—by
an unexpected presence behind the door. He stood rubbing his eyes to see if this figment of his elusive wife
would be wiped away in two strokes of the knuckle.

Sitting on the bed, facing away from the gaping
doorway, Delta Tells was indelible to his credulity. Hooded
in a black shawl that was drawn taut over both shoulders
by hands that must have gathered invisibly in her lap,
she appeared to him as a dense and imperturbable triangle.

But what gripped him in the rigor mortis of surprise was the sound that skipped over the clatter hooves
of his breathing. It was a lullaby chiming from all corners
of the triangle and most conclusively in the rocking
motion that showed him how the base of the triangle was
formed by something slung between Delta's locked el-

bows. The lullaby rose above the rattle of the doorknob still clenched in Brainard Tells' fist. It rose above the pounding of his chest and above the metallic catch in his throat by which he understood that he would not be required to say anything or to take another step into the singing room because it proved the mother's story was untrue. She was at home with her child.

In the knowledge that this was true Brainard Tells was at last free of the burden of telling himself that the story was untrue.

The words that Delta had thrust like bullying fingers into his gut suddenly loosened their knots. The souring taste of those words, curdled at the back of his throat, succumbed to a liquid swallow. The jagged memory of his wife's face when she had uttered those words snapped snugly and smoothly into the labyrinthine furrows of his brain like a puzzle solved.

The lilt of the lullaby brought the pulse of the child's safe existence back into Brainard Tells' consciousness. And not wanting to know how the child had been made to vanish in the first place—or he would have to wonder how it could happen again—he let the fact of the child's rhythmic presence suffice, however schematically indicated by the angular harmonies of the triangle on the bed.

Wordlessly Brainard Tells withdrew to the kitchen, scene of the reputed crime. There he wanted only to let all of his weight settle into the chair that had so provokingly engaged the kitchen table at the moment when the accusation was hurled.

"You have eaten your own."

These words had their own weight from which he thought he could at last extricate "his own," so that whatever else it might be, it would be more than spittle lashed off Delta's tongue.

But no sooner had he felt the old intimacy of the chair warm to the weight of his weary hindquarters than the sound of the lullaby ceased as if in obedience to the rule of a children's game remembered in the image—seen from above—of a shadow-driven figure nervously circling an empty chair. But where he would have been safe in the game, he was now exposed to a sensation of precariousness that could not have been more antithetical to the wide embrace of the chair. All sense of the applicability of rules abandoned him. He felt the certain insecurity of the circus clown whose pants are destined to fall down every time he stands: beltless.

And he shuffled from the kitchen with the pace of a man whose pants have pooled around his shoes. The silence at the end of the hall, like light in a telescope, seemed out of reach. But he knew that he must make the journey.

As he approached the bedroom he felt the breath coming to him as if out of the gradually constricting tube of the telescope, his lung winking at the extremity where his eye should be. It was as if he had walked the wrong way through a foreshortening focal plane that left every sensation miniaturized and intensified in the wake of his passage. When he opened the door each detail of the room sparkled with brittle highlights, shards of the vision from which he had previously taken his comfort whole. He expected to hear the crunch of slivers underfoot as he crossed the threshold of the room, so shattered was the calm he had left behind him there.

Yet when he blinked again he saw that nothing was broken here. Perhaps he had crashed instead through an enormous plate window, mistaking what he saw through it for what it was, curiously blinded to the streaming lacerations that beribboned his body—still moving forward—by the troubling intactness of the objects persisting in his vision: the brass bed still stood upright in the center of the room; the mirror on the far wall showed him his features as if at the bottom of the stillest well; the carpet was not shredded with splinters of the floor buckled beneath it. Above all else, sunlight streamed through the window in long, tensile, unbroken rays. Such radiance could pierce his heart.

Then he salvaged the credulity of his uneasiness with this thought: that if it was not the shattering of the room itself, it was the very unbroken flow of the sunlight that accounted for the silence around which everything seemed to have collapsed like the roof of the mine over its hollow spaces. For where it was still so brightly illuminated on the edge of the bed, the black triangle did indeed appear to have been melted into an amorphous shape no bigger than a large lump of coal. Whatever interior darkness bulked beneath the black wrapping of the shawl, he believed that it was the weight of coal he would ultimately have to shift from his thoughts.

But when Brainard Tells' fingers found the seams of the woolen swaddling, when he opened the black wings which were so tightly folded against a dense mammalian warmth, he was not surprised to discover neither the lump of coal nor the slick, hairy body of a bat, but the ball of wax looking back at him from its iridescent surface with the most penetrating stare.

"Memory wax." He recalled his wife's name for it, as if the name were a pebble buried in the pliant accretions of his own memory, something that could be picked out with a probing finger. The throbbing malleability of the wax, he knew, was not the work of the sun, in the glare of which he still stood stiffly cradling the slippery bundle. Rather, it was the wife's hand in all this that had done the relevant work. And when he examined the specimen more closely in that light, he noticed that it was not the bulging relief of his wife's modelling fingers around the wax, but the clear impress of her face in it that weighed so bodily against his open palms.

He knew it was Delta Tells' own body heat that had glazed the waxen imprint, imparting to the sticky cluster of facial features a sheen as hard and bright as glass. Impulsively polishing that surface with the soft, circular motions of a solitary finger pad—because all shiny surfaces want a body to hold—Brainard Tells suddenly realized that here he touched her open eye. He saw that the breath drawn in through her nostrils had raised two goose bumps against his squeamish touch. Her high cheekbones had made shallow enamelled sinks, almost wet to the touch and a sliver of breath—perhaps a word—extruded between the lips gave an all too palpable taunt to the finger that was already idly picking at the corner of her mouth.

But what expression impressed itself here?

Knowing the history of the wax and all that it contained, because the wife's intimacy with the husband knows no material boundaries—and because the wax smeared to wet transparency between two fingertips was the gesture she made to signify this truth—Brainard Tells did not imagine that he could merely fill this empty form with the fullness of his thoughts and thus unmold the expression on her face—the better to read the meaning of those polished eyes, those flared nostrils, those cheeks, those parted lips, whose edges were already surrendering to the continuous motion of his fingertip.

Nor could he simply hold it up to a mirror in order to cheat concavity of what it robs from the world of rounded objets, because the wax possessed its own mirrory sheen that would reflect a blinding light into any opposite glass. Yet the more he thought he could see by sheer looking, the closer his face—eyes as wide, nostrils as flared, cheeks as rigid—moved toward the elusive recesses of this substance into which he had seen his wife deposit the impressions of valued objects. All had been sealed up like buried treasure by the symmetry of the ball. It was the shape to which the inertia of her working hands devolved as inexorably as any object rolling down a hill.

With his face close enough to put on her face mask without seeing what expression he would be wearing then, Brainard Tells let his own breath fog the mirror of her reflection. The most subtle softening of the wax still released olfactory grains of clover and thistle bloom around which a sensory recognition buzzed vivaciously. It made the breath come faster, the veritable lubricant of a motion by which Brainard Tells finally thrust his own face through the mirror. If only in the instant before contact he might catch a glimpse of the madwoman's facial intent, so ferociously fixed, as he imagined it must have been, upon his own crumpling visage.

When he had assured himself that he might have at least smeared her intentions with the force that had gathered so impetuously in his head, he unstuck himself from the wax. He let it drop, a footprint upon which he could now turn his back with every confidence that he was pointed in the right direction.

Bursting into the long hallway from the bedroom, parting the walls with both hands to clear his path, leaping to every other step in his descent from the front porch of the house, he ran with the forward tilt of a man who wants everything to be in front of him. Yet the air that blew past him in this haste carried back from the tip of his nose—which had gone deepest into the wax—its deepest imprint: the perfumed neck of the flower where the bee dips its head into the crimson dark and brings up gold.

Still bent upon having everything in front of him, Brainard Tells ran with the two iron-grated windows of the sheriff's office focussed in his sights, well before he could see that this was where he was going. And because a man who would have everything in front of him can leave nothing behind, Brainard Tells did not look back.

He wiped his mind clean of all that he had just seen: the more than harmonious triangle, the figment-child rocked by the strains of the mother's lullaby and the even greater deception perpetrated by the malleability of the mother's spite in a lump of wax the size and weight of an infant in swaddling. Now well-smeared with the imprint of his own firery eyes and raging mouth, the wax still tasted upon his trembling lip.

And the taste of the wax contained the murmur of the hive as Delta had related its inner workings to him once when their two heads nestled like bobbling eggs in the moist indentation of a goose-down pillow.

"Do you hear me?" she had whispered, the tinkle of her voice hanging off the lobe of his ear like incongruous jewelry.

"This is the pitch and the level of sound that would not be audible above the buzz of the workers."

Her mouth, melting in his ear had modulated its sound phonetically from s's to z's as if she were bringing up the temperature on a griddle. She had tried to keep the stinging intensity of the z in her voice as she started to picture for him the dance of the workers around their queen.

"Like so many bubbles foaming on a surface of boiling water, each is emitting a separate pulse. But together they are tensing a single muscle over the honeycombed structure of the hive. They do not know how much the honeycomb is like the porous matrix of human bone, especially the thigh bone, drawn," he thought she digressed, *"like an arrow to the bowstring by a muscle that attaches pointedly to the groin.*

"The pronged antlia jabbing the shadows around black bug eyes are actually regurgitating the nectar which they have sucked into the pharynx. This end of the anatomy, perpetually wet with its gummy secretions, is focused on the body of the queen like a light that glistens. It does not shine. At the other end of the body the iron barb of the stinger is combed into the oily sheen of the soft black hairs that are tufted and triangulated below the thorax. The undulations of these six hundred separate bodies raises a plush of fur that sits uneasily on the skin from which it sprouts.

"The bees are swarming, but with such an intense miniaturization of animacular frenzy that the whole configuration could be mistaken for an immovable stillness. Lichen on rock. Whoever puts their hand into the hive at this moment will never be shed of the welts."

When her tongue had finally touched the innermost coil of his ear, Delta Tells was speaking of honey. She had explained how the honey is preserved in its hexagonal compartments even after the hive has departed until, over time, and by the inverse of a digestive process very much like the one that produces the comb from abdominal glands invisible to the naked eye, the honey itself, already a product of one regurgitation, is absorbed back into the wax.

Then Brainard Tells, running at full tilt, understood that the taste of the wax was so galling to him precisely because it had made the water collect in the back

of his mouth, lending an ever more lurid palpability to
the memory of Delta's voice gathering audibly behind
him. Since he was still a man who wanted everything to be
in front of him, he could not tolerate even the momentum
which pushes the runner that much faster forward *because*
it comes from behind. Instead, he consoled himself that
whatever irksome salivation wells in the back of the
throat, regardless what cause the tongue could tell of it,
can also—and by the slingshot torsion of the bucket down
that well—be flung furiously forward.

So he spat. But, running head into the wind, appar-
ently more slowly than the wind—because he was running less vehemently than he had spit—he spat into his
own face.

Would he taste the wax twice, he wondered, if he
lapped the spittle from his cheek? Before this quan-
dary could trouble him for reply, he felt the wetness
shedding tearfully from the crest of his cheekbone,
well beyond the purplish reach of his tongue.

Then Brainard Tells realized what was the trouble:
that everything stuck to him, especially in the most
breakneck forward motion. Everything stuck to him and
doubled on contact. Now he was impressed with the
thought that everything which he imagined was in front
of him was already behind him. He was prepared to admit
that the nature of the wax was all that *was his own*. What
stuck in it *became* it in reverse. Nor was this reflection
becoming to himself, because he knew as well as that what
is absorbed into the momentum of a ball rolling downhill
is inescapably its past, almost before it is before it. And he
knew with a certainty tightening around the crown of his
skull that the slant of that hillside was tilting away from
him in the ball of wax where it had bounced so buoyantly
on his tasting tongue.

Light shone behind the two iron-grated windows
of the sheriff's office when Brainard Tells arrived to see
how much the magnification of light upon the metallic
surface of the grates, the windows flanking the narrow
iron-clad door, and the door lolling open in front of him,
resembled domed polyhedronal eyes and a twitching pro-

boscis: well-met if he were the pucker of sweetness waiting to be kissed in the vortex of the flower.

Insted he was happy enough to sit panting in the
ladder-backed chair the deputies extended to him with
the alacrity of a handshake. As if they had been counting
upon the conviviality of the handshake, the two close-
standing deputies smiled at the curious gypsy disguise of
this man attired in a yellow fringed shirt, striped pants,
red shoes, and at the knowledge that they would not have
to wait for him to speak about it. The two silver stars,
shining against the same midnight blue firmament winked
at each other over Brainard's head, as he started to tell the
particulars of the crime that was curled inside his tongue.

"I envisioned for you the fulfillment of my wife's
bloodiest capacities once before." His speech bore the
stain of deeply held resentment. "But this time I can wash
the blood off your hands too.

"Her's was the hand in the shadow that I know still
hovers over your investigation of a woman found dead at
the bottom of a cement stairwell. How the victim's head
came to be found on the other side of a locked door and
at the bottom of those stairs is a secret to which Delta Tells
holds the key. Take it from her hand."

"And what does this have to do with the child that
disappeared?" The question disturbed the deputy's face
when he asked it, like the first footstep toward total
immersion into a still pool.

Brainard felt the dryness in his voice tug at his
windpipe like something uprooted in the shallow breath
of his reply: "Pluck her hand from the shadows of your
doubt, and you will begin to think that if she is guilty of
one crime, she may be guilty of two."

The bulky cargo of the first wooden crate to be
raised by coal trolley, by crane and pulley from the

bottom of the shaft so perilously known by two names—
"LEOPARDI'S LUCK!" and "CATASTROPHE OF 1931"—
was attenuated to a sharp buzzing sound, as narrow and as
taut as the steel hawser winding voraciously into the
reptilian housing of an old gas engine. The engine stood,
a noisy impresario, in the center of the crowd clogging the
shaftway. Men and women stood so closely together that
all expectation of what was about to be revealed thrilled
through one skin.

The square, flat construction of hardwood framing
strengthened with narrower crossbeams gave no indica-
tion of what it contained except in the groans emitting
from uncured timbers maximally stressed at the high
point of the crate's suspension above the silver tracks. The
yellow crane, through which the hawser was threaded,
prepared to rotate over the flatbed of a waiting truck. All
eyes stayed aloft with the flying cargo. The eyes of the
mining men were all the smaller and more bird-like for
their being stranded above ground and caged in the gyre
of so many blinding rotations of the sun.

They stood squarely under the block-like shadow
of the suspended crate without a ripple of concern jostling their ranks, until the exhaust pipe of the truck
attempting to move into better position brought the
tears to their eyes in mockery of the fear they seemed to
mock.

The letting out of the hawser was more ominously
quiet than the taking of it in. But as the descent began, the
audible release of tension in the framing timbers loosened
the knotted throng below. Though it did not dissipate
their amazement.

They had all visited the bottom of the shaft. They
had all already popped their eyes at the smithereens of
bone fragments that shrouded the true scale of what they
looked upon like a mist dispersing the attention so that,
as the eye slipped from one minuscule point of focus to its
concatenating adjacentcies, there shone a skeletal behemoth bigger than the eye could take in without urging its
body to move into a wider orbit of what was there to be
seen.

Each of them had felt the need to move and, moving in their own bodies, had felt some small tremor of the prehistoric life that was embedded in the floor and wall of a coal cavern large enough to magnify the quaking cry for help sounded by any man who stood alone in the echo chamber of his incomprehension.

Each knew however that only by walking back and forth in front of the excavated ground until one's feet began to drag behind the purposeful nugget of intent glinting from bright eyes, could any man or woman have begun to imp the distance between that head and tail which could be easily charted along the white strings gridding the archaeologists' quadrants, but could only be made to weigh in any convincing relation to the once living beast if all thought about it were given over to trudging on and on.

Though none had taken this journey, they all had put cricks in their necks wondering how its distances could be compassed in the four sides of an obdurately flat and oblong wooden crate suspended above their heads. When it ultimately settled on the truck bed it was without any reverberation through which the watchers might salvage a last chance to put flesh on the bones. Not even a rattle of those bones from the iron truck bed gave the sense of what they were watching a weight of bodily experience that might sit with them after the truck was gone.

But when the realization came that this single crate was just one of innumerable others to come resonating up the trolley tracks in that awful mimicry of the cave-in which signaled the approach of every overladen trolley car in its last ascent, the men's distress at the disparity between the size of a single wooden crate and its too expansively imaginable cargo eased like a cramped foot into a larger shoe size.

At the moment of crescendo, however, the women fluttered against the men's chests. Their ears, unattuned to the scale of such noise, seemed to have been shaken loose from their heads like the first fateful particles of a collapsing roof.

As if in the slippage between the men's ease and the women's agitation, the behemoth seemed to have been loosed from its mysterious confinement. The melee began as a frictional itch that ran through the closely pressed bodies until something larger than them all was compelled to scratch. Perhaps because the roaring ascent of the second trolley car was preceded by an ominous cloud of black dust, the men suddenly saw in the women's stricken faces that what they had taken for a familiar lack of familiarity with the sounds of the mine, might be in fact a mistaken identity. So that the expression of fear which had frozen on those women's faces veritably cracked with the abrupt and violent commotion of the men's bodies scrambling toward the exit.

And then the women believed their own fears. But because it came a beat behind the rhythm of their adrenalin, it required a reaction twice as timely as the hesitation which had preceded it.

Then everyone in motion under the same quaking premonition of collapsing rock and timber and all choking on the same held breath—the terror of inhaling poison gas obstructed the bronchial tubes like a stone sucked down the wrong passageway—grew hopelessly entangled. Arms and legs of different bodies came together and together they uncoiled the tentacles of a monstrous confusion, growing larger and more menacing with each blind hurtle of the mob against the tunnel walls.

Even the ones who had stood at the tunnel's entrance were sucked back by a peristaltic action set up in the struggle of the more desperate ones crowded behind them, who for that reason moved more rapidly toward the open air, and in trampling the ones who were already breathing it, obstructed their own escape. All of the sure to be destroyed, falling together, heard an expulsion of breath rushing before them out of the mouth of the cave. A wave breaking on an unreachable shore.

Of all who then heard what was unmistakably a mother's cry for help rise above the roar of that fateful wave, none reached out toward the child who only too imaginably had been torn from his mother's grip and caught in the cresting panic, because all who might have saved him expected to perish with him. All running, they nevertheless all expected to be overtaken by the world shattering footstep of the granite slab and the dolomite boulder, taking in, with their last breaths, a green whiff of the poisonous gas which had certainly detonated the explosion from the deepest hold of the mine, and which, like a scavanger over a battlefield, would finally pass over the heads of the victims, already pinned under their stones.

But the alarm of the mother's cry persevering through the onslaughts of phantasmic rock and gas, by its mere audibility, attenuated the penultimate moment of survival to an unbearable duration. In such gaps of time hope sparks anew, as deadly in such confinement as the lamp lit in the darkness of expanding gases. And the endurance of the mother's protest, ever enlarging the space of opportunity in which someone might charge to the child's rescue, became a tottering burden of guilt for the self-absorbed and oblivious throng, ever more frantically anticipating their own ever more protracted end, until, by the sheer self-consciousness of this duration, they finally experienced the crushing humiliation of knowing that there had been no cave-in after all. That all the commotion had tremored from their own bodies. That even the child was safe among them and standing at the feet of someone who could lift him above the now calmer sea of heads like a shining trophy.

But the mother's face—all that was still moving in their midst—appeared to have been slapped from cheek to cheek by her own vocal exertions until it had become a beacon of blood. Moving as efficiently as if she followed an unwavering light beam, she seemed in greater need of rescue than the serene child who, as he was being lowered into her arms, was still gazing up, blond and rosy-cheeked.

The blood in the mother's face crested in the blushing cheeks that turned away from her and her child as they pushed their way wordlessly through the shame-faced crowd and into open air.

However anxious not to tempt fate, no one fell in behind the soft step of her departure. Reluctantly remaining behind, under the dark cowling of the mine shaft entrance, so as to be shielded from the indignant mother's stony eyes should she fling them vindictively over her shoulder, the survivors of mock catastrophe found themselves waiting in embarrassment for the sound of the next trolley car, ascending to its crescendo with all the certainty of the gong that strikes the evening meal.

Only after watching the stack of wooden crates rise up on the unflinching back of the truck-bed did the watchers begin to shed their embarrassment in a more intimate attunement of their credulity with the undeniable weight accruing where they had first marveled at its absence: if the rumblings of a single trolley car could unleash the avalanching presence of a violent behemoth, then a behemoth might be contained, however piecemeal, in the minuscular creaking sounds emitted from the cross trees and framing timbers of a flat and oblong wooden crate making contact with the slab bed of a six-ton truck. Upon closer inspection this phenomenon would have been graspable between two fingers—as an inch of compression in the springs of the truck's undercarriage—if one had set the gauge of one's fingertips when the truck was empty.

Those who heard the story with their own ears began to make fists of their brains to beat back prying fingers of credulity.

"Delta tells lies," she said, whose hands, clapped over her ears, made her speech more voluble and the words pout more emphatically on the lips.

"Delta Tells says that a woman is never safe. Her head is prone to the chopping block.

"Delta Tells quickly adds that we ought not to hear a stage whimper in her voice when she says such things because she meant 'prone' as a physical attitude toward the wood. She says she is just speaking factually, as ever.

"Delta Tells asks us if we can feel the place in our own necks where the vertebrae gap like a missing tooth. She says this is where the head is most inclined to bow.

"But I for one am proud of my posture. I can hold my head up high because my neck is straight underneath it. I think of the dark-robed women of the desert who carry all of the water needed to buoy the life of their families on the tops of their unbowing heads, and I know that the physical bearing a woman anoints herself with from the crown of her skull is her most precious possession."

"Delta tells lies," she said, who filled the sockets of her eyes with the soft motion of her two clenched fists as if to blot up the seepage of what she was seeing through the words as she spoke them.

"Delta Tells says that she has been accused of yet another crime. Delta Tells says that she has been connected to a severed head. She asks how a woman may ever be able to make an adequate confession if the crimes are permitted to multiply without her knowledge in advance.

"'So it is always with the woman,' she says, 'that her body is assignable to other places than she herself thinks proper. That a woman has her own mind,' she says, 'is the common delusion of the woman about whom a man has said it, only because he cannot find a way to enter her body. When he finds an opening that bares no teeth against him, he is confident the head is far off. The woman's arms stretched out in the flexure of sexual ecstasy, have set the head rolling.'

"But though I have been told that I have a good head on my shoulders, I *know* it for myself. When I look down at the naked length of my body and mark the place of entry, I judge it to be halfway between my eyes and my toes. There is a number I can divide in half. And when that number comes out of my mouth I close a circuit between the inside and the outside of my being that renders it impervious to all foreign bodies."

"Delta tells lies," she said, who seemed to be slurping the words out of the palm of her hand it was so closely cupped to her lips.

"Delta Tells says that *her* head is on the chopping block.

"Delta Tells says, that her husband has opened a door that stood between the victim's body and the mystery of the head on the other side. Those whom he has invited to bear witness have already walked through that door. Soon their knocking presence on Delta's own doorstep will call for her to open the door.

"'So it is always with the woman,' she says, 'that she is expected to be at home. This is because the husband confuses the woman's with his own body. But where he is well-domiciled in the taut ligature of muscle and bone, she is hung upon that frame like a rag on a stick, if a wind is blowing. So she is the most naked outsider with respect to her own body and most irreconcilably so in the hour of her giving birth. If it is a male child she is only stating the obvious that much more obviously.'

"But I have always been cozy in my body.

"The warmth radiates from a sparkling and multifaceted inner organ that I visualize as ruby red. Basking in its glow I can follow the rays straight back to the center point of my physical being, where I am focussed like the coldest eye that looks out from behind the most securely latched door."

Delta Tells opened the door to the three inquisitors in time enough that the first knock fell silently through the air, already the ghost of its intent. And before the sheriff who had seen his purposeful fist perish before his eyes could summon his tongue to the same purpose, she put the words into his mouth like a rubber stopper.

"Do I know how a head comes to be on the far side of the door which the body never entered?"

Her words held the three intruders in their footsteps like leg-irons tethered to the long shadows that should have clanged loudly behind them where they fell upon the steps of Delta's porch.

"The neck is a remarkable muscle," Delta Tells answered her own question a bit obtusely.

"But," she said, "it is not inaccurate of me to say 'muscle'. Because, though the last twelve vertebrae of the neck—each the size of an inflamed molar—are naturally clenched against the falling weight of the skull, it is the basket-weave of fibrous muscle stretching from the yoke of the collar bone over the crown of the head, that makes it possible to lift the chin sharply, and in that way to tighten the weave until the tension running through it, like a string in its knot, discharges—with a sudden snap of the head—the shudder of any prideful thought."

Because she was that much smaller than her inquisitors, they could not ignore the sharp incline of her chin when they looked for the bottoms of her eyes. Nor could they judge if this was *not* her point.

Tilting her head even more sharply, Delta Tells meant for them to observe the skin thinning over the point of her chin as if she were sharpening a blade somewhere in the recesses of her thought.

"Think of the neck as a vascular conductor and you will begin to appreciate how vulnerable it is with the full engorgement of its tensions. The tighter the cord, the more violent the snap when it is cut.

"Cut the neck and the separate cords will unravel against the head with the force of a rubber band spring-loaded behind its pebble projectile. The head will be carried off in a torrent of energy that seeps and stains as well as spews.

"What thoughts are ejaculated from the head in the arc of its return to earth?" Like an object tossed out of the corner of the eye, this question struck her three auditors quite unexpectedly as one which Delta Tells had no intention of answering herself. And, flustered by the burden of response, they jiggled their throats, loosening the cough of circumspection from its husk of steady breathing.

Because looking at the ever more diminutive figure

of a woman standing in her open doorway gave the three witnesses no access to their thoughts, they turned to face each other exchanging vigorous nods as awkwardly and laboriously as if they were passing one head around the circle of six hands.

Then the one whose mouth Delta had stoppered with the ferocity of her own speech puckered his lips as if to spit out a disgusting morsel indistinguishable from something he wanted to say.

But Delta's jaws peremptorily seized the air between them as if to finish chewing what he refused to ingest. She was already across the threshold of the door through which the others had sought admittance, because when the sheriff had backed up several steps to collide with his companions—though it was something in her face that had startled him backwards—he seemed to have dragged her with him. Now they might have been two dogs tied together by the rag of meat they tore between them.

"Here is your answer," her voice raged out of all proportion to her body, letting it lash behind her like a broken leash.

"The head is its own thought apart from the body, and that is what makes it fall like any other object dropped into space.

"And yet I, of all people, shouldn't need to say that the leverage of one body against another would not be even my method of last resort. Have I not already confessed to you that my method is digestion? Though digestion is like the body it is *not* the body more than any other thought about the body *is* the body.

"So I say again that digestion is my method because I have no patience for the space in which we have to wait for things to happen, the space where bodies collide."

Delta Tells had backed her accusers up against the unbalustraded edge of the wooden porch. Their shadows were foreshortened into dense blobs on the steps that fell away to the street below them. For a moment the tension between the bodies and their shadows waited to be plucked by Delta's purpose. But it was her whole hand that suddenly grabbed the slack folds of the sheriff's belly for the keynote of what she wanted to say.

"I have a head for digestion," her speech roiled into his reddened face. "Here is where the blood fires the engines of bodily appetite," her words followed her fingers. "The capillaries netted around the stomach know something about what the inside wants from the outside which the body can't allow: Osmosis! If thoughts could flow in and out of the body as easily as the gristly meat of digestion permeates the stomach's translucent walls, we would think about things that happen to the flesh in such a way that it would make them happen.

"Is that what you have done? Or is that what you think that I have done to you?

"Consider the slippery similarity between the rolling head and the hard round of a full stomach which got the ball rolling. Tell me which feels more welcoming to the grip of your two hands?"

The sheriff felt his stomach's release like a blow to the steady weight of the rest of his body, at the same moment that he observed Delta Tells' empty hand re-enter the orbit of her own center of gravity. But now the hand was a fist pounding against her rigid flank. The last thing she had to say seemed to be tolled from her torso by the blows of that fist.

"Remember, I have a head for digestion. With it I have put my own child into my husband's belly. But if I have put the thought of decapitation into your heads in the same manner that you believe I perpetrated that first ingestion, then you must disbelieve them both. As you have already judged, such thoughts are strictly of the head and not of the body. Or this is what you thought when I first told my story, even after I had made the words carry the weight of my deed like a body from the bloodiest altar."

The flutter of Delta's fist, coming back to roost over these words, sent the man standing closest to the precipice of the porch steps tottering backwards. As though the balance lost to the rest of his body could be recaptured in the palm of his hand, the falling man seized the shoulder of the one in front of him. As the second man's weight was carried off on the tense wings of the first one's desperation, he grasped the shoulder of the sheriff in turn.

Because the sheriff was the last into the air, his eyes widening as if in proportion to the expanded view that comes with an ascent, he saw that what had appeared to be the unfurling of Delta's fist was in fact the opening of her hand to reveal what could only be a yellowing, desiccated and rindlike morsel of flesh.

But because he was in fact fathoming a descent with no hope of ascension, the sheriff's thoughts shriveled to the recognition that this was the remnant of an umbilical knot: the full lips of the womb drawn to the first pucker of the grave by exposure to the drying air. Detached, no less than a fruit fallen from ripeness.

The wax ball nestled in the trough of the wooden cradle, rocking still—so her husband was convinced— from Delta's last touch. If the rocker blades had been cut to resemble slivers of moon, the wax ball portended the sun where it shone above the topmost slat of the rocker-box like a nodding baldpate. The gravity shedding from its glossy crown was the force that sustained the side to side motion of the box, as if the ground were continuously rolled out of from under it to induce a telepathic tapping of the wax ball against the alternately ringing sideboards of the cradle.

Because no one had seen the provoking hand alight from the bough of the cradle's wooden frame, one could have imagined that the movement of the wax ball, because self-perpetuating, was self-causing as well. So it is that roundness seems to be the cause of its own rolling.

Gripping his head in his hands, as if to save it from

the wave action of the cradle, Brainard Tells tried to surmise if Delta had launched the cradle thinking that the comparable weight of the wax might rock the child back into her imaginative embrace, or if she had taken the real child into her arms in order to make room for the wax.

Halfway across the room Brainard stiffened to listen for footsteps ebbing elsewhere in the house, perhaps reverberating back from a last contact with the cradle, the double beat of which had drawn his own footsteps, returning him to this chamber of deceptions like a watery reflection of himself in the mirror of remembering. Taking another step toward the cradle, he felt the familiarity of his presence in this room catch about his face and hands like cobwebs of time.

Then, breaking the rhythm of the cradle with the heavy contact of one hand, he felt as if he were arresting the hands of a clock at the moment of its striking the next hour. Still, when Brainard Tells seized hold of the smooth grain in the wood it made the wax ball strike the opposite panel of the rocker-box with yet another beat of the drum. It was that much more energy than the inertia already denied to it by this intervention in the laws of equal and opposite forces.

He knelt to it and the bend of his back made the stomach pop out, that much more bulbous above the rim of his belt.

Because the wax ball seemed more glistening than usual, he tilted closer on the balls of his feet to see himself inspecting a perfectly limpid semblance of his own face shining up at him as if out of an oceanic mirror stretched across the curvature of the globe. His ears pinned back by the convexity of that gaze were opposite land masses between which his eyes floated uncertainly.

When he placed his hands over the ears he had a grip of that world as firmly, or so he thought, as if he had made it with the same hands. But, because he realized that touching it was indistinguishable from smearing its contours, he opened his hands flat enough that his palms made only the slightest contact with its radiant curvature.

By then he realized that the wax ball was shinier than usual because it was slicker than usual. It could have come directly from the salivating jaws of some carnivorous gargantua grown impatient with rolling it between the bloodless rows of teeth.

What cannot be chewed must be spit out, Brainard Tells thought, as the wax ball slipped from his grip.

The reflection of his eyes that glittered off the surface, and into the gyration of a marble shot from the hollow of a child's moist palm, was his only bead on this involuntary action.

Then it was the crack in the substance that gave what should have merely flattened into a misshapen pancake the look of an egg where it slapped the floor between Brainard Tells' splayed and involuntarily dancing feet. The crack in the wax ball was the ragged silhouette of the biting jaw which might have spit it, but the interior of the egg was what drew Brainard's vision.

The insertion of one finger into the crack, ruffled the darkness cleft between the fissured walls of wax.

Then, because he had placed his finger where the pupil of his eye would have gone had it followed this line of sight to the dotted object of his attention—and which in turn would have centered the floating white of his eye—he felt as if he had poked himself in the eye. This blind spot was the broken yoke of the egg when the force of his probing fingertip liquified, a ticklish sensation that he now considered could only be the hairs, so eerily tufted on a bee's back. The black he had spotted in the vertex of the white crevice could have been nothing else but the sweet-toothed insect that bites.

And now the more gingerly touch that he conferred at the center of the imperfectly orbed wax brought the insect into more tactile focus: the double set of veined, translucent wings notched together just above the thorax, the once buzzing air between the wings thickened to a silent butter from its struggle to fly free, the six legs like iron struts seized upon by a quicksand. And beneath the thoraxical pelt the pointed absence of the poison barb bodied forth a dense and obdurate stillness that was, he inferred from the shiver of warmth it gave off, the most frenziedly concatenated motion of the insect's last jabbings into a soft and insatiably receptive matter.

The vividness of all that was here came as if his fingertip were padding over the blind surface of his eye, bringing out the shape of the segmented body like a fossil intaglio from the smoothest stone.

But instead he realized that what was contained in the wax ball could only have been so implanted if the insect had alighted upon a flattened surface. Brainard Tells knew that every globe divides into two flatter hemispheres. His brain mapped itself onto this consciousness as if the thought were a hand smoothing out a sheet of paper in front of the lines running so quickly upon it. He saw the ball flat. In this case the two hemispheres would have been made one by a gesture identical to clapping closed the resounding covers of a heavy book. Hooking his straight thumbs into the crevice between the waxen halves, Brainard Tells pried open the book as if he were breaking a succulent meat from its shell.

Then he saw with his eye what his finger had not revealed to touch: that the bee trapped in the wax held its own prey to its breast and that the mechanism of the embrace was not the six bent iron legs, but the saber wisp of the stinger which he had at first believed to be lost in the wax like a drop of water in a lake of ice, but which was mated to the lower body of a blue-eyed housefly in such a way as to make a curious encirclement of the two atavistically joined bodies.

But then Brainard Tells looked again: this time using his eye as if it were a magnifying lens in the grip of hovering fingers and attempting to find the proper alignment between the socket in the inclining head and the shockingly enlarged specimen which bumped against the lens of this scrutiny like the horizon hurtling through the windshield of a speeding automobile. It was neither one insect or two that finally jumped upon the darting focus of his black pupil like a water bug rippling the surface tension which holds its own image beneath it.

Instead what appeared in Brainard's vision now

was nothing less than a human eyeball. Half-sheathed in the elasticity of its upper lid, it mirrored the illusion of bodily segmentation where the rippling edge of skin lost its grip on the jellied protuberance of fear gleaming whitely away from it. Seeing that it was tufted with long lashes on the bulging meridian, where the lid bisected the curvature of this milky globe, Brainard Tells understood how his touch had been so mistaken. What could be otherwise a bee was *not*, anymore than a fingertip could be an organ of sight.

Further disentangling the resemblances between one sense and another he also saw that the muscles which would have held the rolling eyeball in the orbit of the brain had been cut. Shriveled stubs adhered symmetrically around the shiny perimeter so as to suggest the momentous markings on a clock face. The only resemblance that still tickled his fingertip to think of the vanished insect was the small size of the eye which would have fit the face of a doll.

So, staring into the cleft ball of wax to meet the severed gaze of the doll, Brainard Tells caught again the reflection of his most gruesome imagination, fatefully returned to the still agitated pool in which he had first contemplated the wife's worst proclaimed deed. It struck him with a certainty that made him forget how the eye is a pool of water as well, that flexes against what it sees as palpably as the thrown stone, though the stone now seemed to shimmer up at him from the bottom of his being.

Where she hovered silently and invisibly above her husband's head, at the top of the house, Delta Tells let the sloping planes of the attic roof fall over her crouching shoulders like wings holding the musty warmth of this perch, keeping it safe for the hatching.

The folio-sized volume lay unbalanced in her lap, all its pages pushed back to front so that it opened upon the last glassine-glistening view of the body. The viewer entered this book through the mouth. She would be satisfied to leave it through the anus.

Then the page was turned. The glass was broken. But the true depth of the glassine surface, like a self-replenishing spring, remained to be seen. The epidermal layer which gave to the manifest density of the buttocks the appearance of breath building up to a warble behind puffy cheeks, gave way in turn to a flatter whorl of musculature concentrating around the anal orifice the look of an angry red eye.

Catching the slick surface of the page with the grit of a chipped fingernail and picking at an edge of the sphincter's indigo aureole, Delta Tells felt the tension necessary to turn the page again quicken in her knuckle like a snake rising from the charmer's basket. The finger moved, in as straight a line, though its motion was strictly horizontal.

Another page. And because the pressure of the finger at that point would have sufficed to etch a line in glass, the stiff, plastic page had made a snapping sound as it turned. What had first appeared to be the smallest of openings had, upon the turning of the page, transpired into a glowering tunnel lined from top to bottom with a plush of livid tissue. It had become a more predatory orifice. The length of the tunnel could not be judged from the viewer's myopic vantage. But in the adjustment of her eye to the darker palette of the internal organs, Delta Tells discerned how the tunnel was subtly ribbed with cords of muscle, not unlike the regularly placed timbers which shored the walls of the mine shaft against upheavals from below.

Stiffening her finger in the raw eye of the tunnel, she made one joint flex against another so as to snap the page again, as if it were a spell that could be broken. But here, where she might have preferred the puff of blue smoke, the unveiling of a golden-crowned prince, husked of his frog's body, there was only the last page of the book.

The comparatively flat planes of hip-bones and pelvis could not have more severely belied the pneumatic convexity of the buttocks which had preceded them.

But unlike every other contact with the bone offered up to the viewer in this book, this last was not a paper page to be dredged from the glassine depths. Instead the two symmetrical halves of the pelvic bone—they resembled nothing so much as the skull cleft with an axe—adhered to their own clear plastic pane. For this reason what was the endpaper of the book and clearly no part of the body, shone through to illuminate what, planted firmly in the flesh, would have been otherwise black as coal to the body-blinded eye.

And so, once again, with the simple turning of a page, the viewer could pass through the limit of the body's density as if into an expansive blue sky which was the color that suffused the considerable width of the book's recto endboard, to which the square of blue paper was forever glued.

R eawakening the rocking motion of the cradle with his right foot and following the sorrowful rhythm of the empty rocker-box with his bobbing head—as if giving perverse assent to its emptiness—Brainard Tells moved his hands to embrace the sickness that was just stirring in his belly. He had no sea legs for the voyage he was embarked upon now.

The whitecaps of his queasiness frothed to a boil. A drowning body struggled amidst the turbulent cloud of bubbles that rises effortlessly to an unattainable surface from flaring nostrils and gaping mouth. Limbs tangled among the entrails where Brainard Tells felt his own center of gravity plunge precipitously. But the spasm which at that moment doubled him up upon himself also told him—with the unquestionable authority of an unexpected blow—that the center of gravity was no longer *his own*. And because he was now staring at his own gut through the gaze turned upside down—the blow might have taken his head off altogether—he could see that however encompassing the embrace of his arms around his struggling midriff, what they held was no longer in their grip.

From the moment of its birth, everyone had said that the child's face was only his own. Now Brainard Tells could not even own the sensations which blurred this memory of what he longed to confirm. They were like the water into which the face inadvertently splashes the more closely it comes to inspect the resemblances proffered from a reflective surface. Still bent over, as he was, he imagined the slipperiness of the damp bank upon which one finds such illusory purchase.

As if out of obedience to that recrimination he went easily to his knees. In that motion the distance between his stomach and his face collapsed into his hands. Now, because the wetness in his palms was nothing for him to see, and because he could not resist the urge to taste it—nauseating as it promised to be—he accepted the eviction from his body which, in previous bouts with the peristaltic strongman trampling his gut, he had just as violently opposed.

Now he thought it might after all be true that he had eaten his own: all that was his own was *now*. The moment shuddered through him, a retreating wave carrying on its crest the body which had desisted from its struggle with unknown depths. And though it filled his mouth, the regurgitation tasted like nothing at all. The memory of salt was as wet on his cheek as it was dry on his tongue after the last heaving. But he did not claim it as *his own*.

Bereft as it was of its contents, he could now contemplate the slackened rope of his stomach, as one who dangles from the barest rafter of his thoughts.

What could lift such dead weight from its fatal abyss but the hands that now duly reached down between his legs and took up from the floor the wax ball so provokingly fissured by the impact of its original fall? What could carry such a dead weight off its tragic hook, but the rolling momentum of the ball that now turned impatiently under Brainard Tells' impatient feet?

It occurred to Delta Tells, contemplating the charges against her, that the thought of decapitation— only her husband could have conjured it into the heads of the authorities—was perversely symmetrical with the roundness of that aching belly which she, for her part, had fitted to his head like the infamous iron mask of medieval torture. It was true, she judged harshly, that people always found the worst things in themselves to love in others. "Only in that way can we be assured that such frailties will get the punishment they deserve."

This was the sentiment that tethered her to her own memory of being led by resonant footsteps through a labyrinthine night, a pathway of rain-slicked streets reflecting nothing but the darkness that pooled in their puddles, the gurgling of a drain at the end of the path, the certainty that even the drain which always leads below ground was in this case well below ground itself, that every footstep craving absorption into the shape she shadowed and which was the seal of her secrecy was, potentially, a step into the abyss.

But she had halted her steps out of anger, not out of fear. The stark nakedness of her footfall, exposed by the silence that had fallen dead ahead of her, stiffened her into a pose of garden statuary, half turned toward some action in the world which has long since been completed by others. Even more infuriating, the reason why she felt trapped in this pose burst upon her in a resonant chord of labored breathing which seemed to be imminently under-foot, despite the fleetness with which she had broken her stride. Heavy breathing and the succulence of parting lips.

In the next moment she felt exhaled from the moment, and by that expulsion of bodily warmth, loosed from the cold bond of her silence, broken out of the marble pose of her secret presence in the dark night. She felt free to move toward the aura of light shimmering up to her from what she knew to be the dangerously inclined cement stairwell where her husband had vanished. She knew that she herself would evade discovery if, inching closer to the horizon of the topmost stair, she took the requisite precautions of the seer who does not wish to be seen, and did not try to rise above it.

Though she was standing perfectly erect as she approached what would have been the threshold of visibility seen from the bottom of the stairwell, she felt her whole body concentrated into the pinpoint of focus that makes peeping over a darkling edge a matter of infinitesimal adjustments in the dilated pupil. She could only permit herself to move close enough that the horizontal line of the topmost step might come into perfect alignment with the lower lid of the eye where the pupil perched with such predatory alertness. In that way, she would still be shrouded in invisibility while the two figures below her, already joined in an embrace that unfurled a phoenix-like wingspan, stood out in flaming silhouette. What was etched so fiercely by the light that burned above the door at the bottom of the stairwell was the image of her husband, now rising to the ascent which the other woman had already attained in his embrace and ironically by the support of the very grip upon the handrails which he now loosed into the air.

Now Delta Tells followed the descent of the disfigured bird by crossing the horizon of her spywatch. Her toes hooked talon-like over the topmost step, she could see what the force of gravity had done below her as if she had ascended upon the very wingspread beneath which her husband and the other woman appeared to have collapsed.

Only from this vantage point could the accident be explained. The husband's releasing his grip upon the handrails had sprung loose the full weight of the woman's

body, arched and so that much more treacherously canti-
levered upon the male erection. Cantilever was as a result
converted into catapult. The counterweight of its pay-
load—the man frantically, and so mistakenly, refinding
his grip on the woman's fear-straightened legs instead of
on the iron handrails—fell upon her, driving her head
first towards the glass pane already trembling in its wooden
door frame at the bottom of the stairwell.

Delta Tells heard in the sound of splintering glass
the fortuitous splash of the fish, wriggled free of the
eagle's talons. Now she was the bird soaring obliviously
above the, once again, impenetrably still waters of its depth-
bound quarry.

Brainard Tells, by now a man who believed that
he might never be able to desist from his running, arrived
once again, and even more breathlessly than before, at the
door of the sheriff's office, his steps frothing and pooling
about his feet like the aftermath of a cresting wave. This
time the door was shut. Through the glass pane that bore
letters denoting an officialdom within and which were
painted upon a rippling surface, he saw, as if through
troubled water, shapes in motion, moving toward him.

Then he made what he thought was the reciprocat-
ing gesture, giving way to the tide of urgency that had
brought him this far—bearing the evidence of the eyeball
still orbed in wax—so that he now watched himself proffer the wax ball straight through the glass pane and so
through the shut door.

To those who watched incredulously from the
other side—the sheriff and two deputies—the breathless
runner, glistening in an effervescent halo of glass shards,
had the look of a man coming up for air from a drowning
depth.

Through a spray of blood, Brainard Tells at first

could not see how he had blinded himself to what was being proffered in his direction from the other side of the glass, by obtruding the very object that he now held at the fullest extension of his own lacerated arms. He held it beyond the barrier of the door where his feet had nonetheless been belligerently halted. But because he had already passed through the glass, though his toes still stubbed numbingly against the skirt of the door, and because the first of the two deputies, who had flanked the sheriff behind his desk, had then moved expeditiously out in front of that desk, ready to receive what Brainard Tells made to offer, he was at last prepared to release himself into the custody of anyone whose wide-opening arms might at least carry him off his stymied feet, leaving the last of the physical barriers behind.

When Brainard Tells looked up again—somehow he had already passed through the door as well as through its clear pane—he finally saw what he had unwittingly denied himself sight of by the very obdurateness of what he had insisted upon showing the sheriff first.

"A bee," proclaimed the first deputy, scrutinizing the wax ball received out of the donor's hands on the mirror side of that identical gesture by which Brainard Tells now saw: what had been hidden behind this wax blind only a moment ago, was revealed—like an angelic head bursting from its iridescent corona—to be an infant caressed in blue swaddling, dusted with golden stars and exuding the pinkness that casts upon all other colors a deathly pallor.

"A baby," retorted Brainard Tells in a tone of voice as flat as the hand with which the first deputy had laid the bee-rounded orb upon the hard sheen of the sheriff's mahogany desk.

Now, cradled as much in the ministrating arms of the second deputy as the infant was cradled in the arms of the sheriff, Brainard Tells understood that he could not reach out and touch what was at last so tantalizingly graspable by his own impalpable and doubt-beleaguered mind. For this reason he would have to content himself with merely hearing an *account* of the astonishing facts confronting him, which he was confident that the sheriff's rasping voice would raise, like so many foul weather warning flags, above the infant's inconsolable squalling. Thus Brainard Tells might even make a virtue of necessity, better to resist the temptation to touch what is inevitably the taunt of all emptyhandedness.

Seated on a low chair that made him feel as though he might be kneeling before the sheriff's desk and looking past the red cross emblazoned upon the first-aid box—it had burst open upon the desk from the excesses of gauze and cotton wadding with which the second deputy now attended to his wounds—Brainard Tells discerned in the brawny figure of the sheriff, cuddling the infant to his own brightly starred breast, the paradox of a bearded madonna who could be both merciful and cruel. Her kiss would be both warm and scratchy.

The sheriff spoke first of the woman who had delivered the infant into his arms. She had whispered to him under purple eyelids. Her turbaned head sprouted a languorous peacock feather. The confetti patchwork of her gown was streaked with the sauces that might have bubbled over the rim of a cook pot high enough for the stirrer to stand up inside of it herself, armored with cast iron to her waist. Her cheeks blushed with smudges of coal smoke which puffed out the redder cheeks of the fire below. So she was a woman of the open road.

Holding her palm up before the sheriff's most quizzical face, as if to show him a map of her adventures, she had made the tip of his index finger walk the wavering length of her lifeline to the place where she claimed to have discovered the child.

Even the inveterate walker on the road—who has witnessed every trespass of credulity—had been surprised to hear the whimpering stones. Where there was no crossroad and the way was as straight as an accusatory finger, it would have been surprising enough for the walker to come upon a pyramidal cairn, so conspicuously a marker neither of direction or mileage. But it defied the experience of the walker altogether to hear the bleat of a human suckler emanating as it did from a conical pile of stones which stood by the side of the road and

*which measured, if nothing else, the distance from the ground
to her knees.*

*The sound which had caught the walker's attention
carried in a vibration from one stone to another so that its
distinct undertone evoked the industrious buzzing of the hive.
Then stooping to the sound, the mysterious walker felt a
movement in the stones that was something more than sound,
though something less than the quaking of an egg when the
moment of hatching is upon it.*

*In the palm of her hand the first stone seemed heavy
enough to have been thrown through the air. As if it had fallen
on her heart she moved quickly to remove one after the other
of the remaining stones until she thought that in her haste she
might have dug a hole straight through the earth: so twinkling
was the sky in which her hands suddenly floated helplessly
above their purpose. The firmament with all its stars shone
through to her before a single infantile limb could give a
purchase on the rescue she had so urgently intended, because
the infant had been swaddled for this burial, and in a blanket
which contoured the very cosmos to the unexpected plumpness
of a body which (the walker surmised) might have cushioned
the blow of the most vehemently cast stone.*

*And the cheshire smile which shone from behind the
last flat stone, that should have smashed the miniature porcelain to powder, widened the walker's eyes until she felt it had
imparted a roundness to her being, upon which, she assured
the sheriff (as she departed), she floated still.*

Holding forth the ample roundness of the infant as
if he intended it to be a considerable weight that would
not float lightly upon the father's outstretched and intricately bandaged arms, the sheriff did not even solicit
confirmation that this was in fact the missing child of
whom the father had spoken so ominously, and as it
turned out, on an empty stomach. One whose thoughts
floated so buoyantly, the sheriff surmised, would need
the ballast.

For this reason the sheriff made the act of passing
the child over the top of his desk the bearer of stern
questions that fell like stones upon Brainard's smiling
face.

"If the mother is *not* the unnatural criminal, who is the father to say so?

"If the absence of the child is the reason for the father's presence, what fateful sway does the presence of the child in the father's arms hold over the mother's absence?

"If the mother is *not* guilty of the act born of the husband's ignorance of the facts, what guilt is born of the act about which he claims to have knowledge?

"In other words," he asked, in words that were not audibly other, "what guilt is *borne*?"

Then, as if the sheriff feared that the ensuing silence grew from the absence of the distinction which he had himself called into being by his careless choice of words, he spoke with more tidy circumspection. "Or, if the elegant inversions of my questioning seem to depend too much upon a verbal convolution that pretends to fill a space which it in fact only makes bigger and emptier, let me ask you plainly: *where is your wife?*"

It amused Brainard Tells to think that the woman who prompted the question, so ludicrous in the disguise of a gypsy sorceress, was herself the answer to the question.

So ludicrous was the naivete of the man who asked the question, that he could not tell the disguise from what it told him.

Before Brainard Tells could reconnoiter his way home, prepared to strip off the last of his wife's disguises, prepared to brandish the miraculously intact body of the infant like the sword of an avenger, he was himself struck down in the street by the news of Delta Tells' disappearance. It fell upon him from a window: three protruding heads chiming together a single voice. He was accosted in the twisting of a narrow lane that daily led this trudging pedestrian to lose sight of his destination for several steps just before it ushered him directly to his front door. This familiar but no less torturous turning of the way was, for Brainard Tells, the loop through which the string pulls tight its knot and which always brought to his mind the first kink of intestinal pain that is the portent of greater abdominal distress. In this blind spot of his progress toward home Brainard Tells was forced to see what he refused to bear witness to, though he was admonished by the three heads to go and see for himself.

Where the most portentous entrance to the mine bore out the cryptic common sense of its two names—LEOPARDI'S LUCK!" and "CATASTROPHE OF 1931"—in a sharp divergence of the shaftways, a solitary guard had noticed a gap in the iron- barred entrance to the mine's most long abandoned vein. The locks, cut from their chains and as big as the heads of dolls, had fallen in the dust. The guard saw how they gave voice to the scream of all precipitous falls through their gaping keyholes rounded, to his eyes, in awful mimicry of the mouth aghast. For three hundred yards beyond the narrowly parted gate—the blink of an eye would have let it slip right through his notice—a raw and grimly exposed mountain crag told the story of the stone floor once giving way without warning into a rushing underground river. Here on the lip of the disaster, where he ordinarily would have said that the cries of the miners plummeting so long ago were audible still, the guard discovered a small pile of clothes, lightly stirring as if a shallow breath ran through them. A feathered turban, a patchwork gown, a hand-sized mirror flecked with what looked like the spatterings from a simmering cook pot, a whiff of coal-smoke.

If Brainard Tells had been able to blow upon the embers of intent which still seemed to be breathing here, he might have rekindled the flame of understanding. Instead, on hearing this reporting of the facts, Brainard Tells felt the infant stir against his breast with a strength that might have burst the iron cage of his ribs. And then the cries erupted like the howling of a wild beast gripped in the tersely silent jaws of a sprung trap. The victim quickly realizes that the wide open mouth is no match at all for the trap, except that it opens the head to knowledge of the body as an empty and wind-swept place.

Those who heard the story with their own ears suffered the sound to be rendered into such a torrent of water that it drowned out any other voice than her own.

"Delta tells lies...," she said, who drew her lower lip into her mouth like a breakwater against the grief of the tongue.

"Delta Tells lies in the middle of the swiftest current that can flow through rock, as ever, a swimmer against the stream. So she has found her way to a place where the husband has no hold, neither finger nor toe, because the body in perpetual motion is the solution into which all the most possessive thoughts are ineluctably dissolved."

"Delta Tells lies...," she said, whose eyes were brimming with what she could not see, though she knew it without a doubt.

"Delta Tells lies like one more stone beneath the mounting harvest of stones that have washed to the mouth of the river in endless regurgitation of what it has swallowed. It is a fitting entombment for a woman who has so bravely endured the stoniness of the husband's response in the softest and most impressionable parts of her fleshly existence."

"No," she said, who was the last to speak, "Delta Tells lies in the rattling flatbed of the bonneted gypsy wagon, with the road bucking in her thighs and the passage into her body become a path upon which her husband's footsteps will forever clatter after her. For the man who lies between her legs now wears a skin that is a shade of her husband's shadow, where it is already beating the road like a stick in his hapless pursuit.

"Delta Tells is conceiving again, but this time in the flesh that feels no necessity to speak of what it means to lay the body down."